BOOK TWO: THE DEEP

DIVE

**A world of adventure from
Gordon Korman**

DIVE

BOOK ONE: THE DISCOVERY
BOOK TWO: THE DEEP
BOOK THREE: THE DANGER

EVEREST

BOOK ONE: THE CONTEST
BOOK TWO: THE CLIMB
BOOK THREE: THE SUMMIT

ISLAND

BOOK ONE: SHIPWRECK
BOOK TWO: SURVIVAL
BOOK THREE: ESCAPE

www.scholastic.com

www.gordonkorman.com

GORDON KORMAN

BOOK TWO: THE DEEP

DIVE

AN
APPLE
PAPERBACK

SCHOLASTIC INC.
New York Toronto London Auckland Sydney
Mexico City New Delhi Hong Kong Buenos Aires

ISBN 0-439-50723-5

12 11 10 9 8 7 6 5 4 3 2 1   3 4 5 6 7 8/0

Printed in the U.S.A.   40

First printing, July 2003

For Spencer and Harrison Newman

DIVE

29 August 1665

The sword was the smallest that could be found aboard the Griffin, yet thirteen-year-old Samuel Higgins could barely lift it with both hands.

"But what am I to do with this, sir?" the cabin boy asked in alarm.

York, the ship's barber and surgeon, regarded him sternly. "We're going into battle, Lucky. You won't be picking your teeth with it."

Samuel was aghast. "Me? I'm to join the fight?"

The word had spread like wildfire through the English privateer fleet that the invasion of Portobelo was at hand. This was what they had crossed the perilous Atlantic for, losing fully a third of their number to scurvy, fever, and the malevolent sea. At the end of this day lay riches beyond their wildest dreams.

In a secluded inlet, forty miles north of the treasure city, the nine remaining privateer ships lay at anchor. Each vessel was manned by a skeleton crew. The majority of the English seamen were loaded onto a flotilla of twenty-four canoes. These had been car-

2

ried all the way from Liverpool for exactly this purpose — a sneak attack on Portobelo.

Hugging the coast, the canoes were paddled
south, rushed along by the fast-moving current. Each
narrow craft was about forty feet long and equipped
with a small sail. The assault force totaled about five
hundred in number. They were led by the captain of
the Griffin, the dreaded corsair James Blade.

"Row, you scurvy scum!" the captain roared.
"We reach Portobelo before dawn, or your bodies
will lie at the bottom of the bay!"

Struggling with a heavy oar, Samuel knew this
was not an empty threat. Over the course of their terrible journey, he had seen Blade strike, flog, and even
hang his crew. And the cruel captain had murdered
Evans, the sail maker, Samuel's only friend aboard
the barque. The memory of that good man's terrible
end still caused the boy to well up with suppressed
anger.

By the time they had covered the forty-mile distance, Samuel's hands were raw and bleeding. He
wasn't sure he would be able to clutch his sword,
much less defend himself with it.

Blade indicated a pattern of flickering lights in
the moonless blackness ahead. "The torches of Santiago Castle! Muffle the oars! We'll take those fancy
dons by surprise!"

No sooner had the words passed his lips than gi-

ant signal fires flared, illuminating the stone fortress before them. There was a flash, followed by a huge explosion. A split second later, a cannonball sizzled over their heads, close enough for Samuel to feel its hot wind. It struck the water behind them, sending up a steaming geyser.

"To the beach!" howled Blade, standing in the bow, a cutlass in one hand and his bone-handled snake whip in the other. "If you want to line your pockets with Spanish gold, first stain your swords with Spanish blood!"

The battle had begun.

THE DEEP

CHAPTER ONE

Perhaps one diver in a thousand would have noticed the faint glimmer on the ocean floor. Dante Lewis spotted it immediately.

Silver!

Heart racing, he deflated his buoyancy compensator (or B.C.) vest and began to descend toward it, passing towering coral formations and clouds of sea life.

The Hidden Shoals off the Caribbean island of Saint-Luc boasted some of the most spectacular colors on the face of the earth — the brilliant turquoise of a parrot fish, the electric magenta of red algae, the neon yellow of a snapper's tail, the shimmering violet of a school of Creole wrasses.

Dante perceived none of it.

That wasn't exactly true. He could see everything — and far sharper than the average person. But only in black and white and shades of gray.

The promising thirteen-year-old photographer was *color-blind*. That was why he had accepted the diving internship at Poseidon Oceanographic

DIVE

Institute. Not to *learn* color — his brain wasn't wired for that. But maybe he could learn to detect it, figure it out from the clues he *could* see — light, dark, and shading.

He checked the Fathometer on his dive watch to see how deep he'd gone. Forty feet.

So far, the plan was a dismal failure. Descending in full scuba gear, Dante swung around his Nikonos underwater camera to snap a picture of a flamingo tongue — a rare spotted snail, supposedly orange on peach. To Dante, it appeared gray on gray.

Everything is gray on gray, he reminded himself glumly. *And it always will be.*

Sixty feet. He looked down. The glint of silver was still far below.

Dante felt he was stuck on a backward island in the middle of nowhere for the whole summer. There was nothing to do but dive, an activity that he wasn't much good at, and liked even less. He had almost gotten himself killed at least once already.

And for what? Gray fish, gray plants, gray coral.

But there was money in these waters. From centuries of sunken ships. Dante and his companions had already found an antique Spanish piece of eight. His brow clouded. The three-hundred-year-old coin had been stolen from them by their supervisor, Tad Cutter. The interns would not make the mistake of trusting the slick Californian again.

Eighty feet. It was deeper than he had ever been, but he barely gave it a second thought. He was completely focused on reaching the source of the glimmer.

And then his flippers made contact with the soft sandy bottom. He peered down at the object that had drawn him to the depths.

A 7UP can.

His disappointment surged like the clouds of bubbles that rose from his breathing apparatus.

Stupid, he berated himself. It was crazy to believe that every glint in the ocean was some kind of lost treasure. *But it would have been sweet to snag a pile of silver and rub it in Cutter's face!* The institute man had done a lot more than swipe one little coin. He and his team had taken over the wreck site it had come from.

They're probably over there right now, digging up our discovery!

It was a huge rip-off, no question about it. Yet the whole business didn't seem to bother Dante right then. Instead he felt pretty good. A dull, pleasant fatigue, like a runner's high.

Funny — he was normally pretty nervous on a

dive. Underwater seemed like a place that people simply weren't meant to be. But now he was starting to feel confident. Fearless, even.

A curious lionfish ventured close — a mass of spines and fins and stripes.

It's an underwater porcupine in designer clothes!

In some remote corner of his mind, it occurred to Dante that he should take a picture. But he made no move for the Nikonos tethered to his arm. Instead, he reached out to touch an elaborately striped fin.

The attack came from above, knocking him backward. His dive partner, fourteen-year-old Star Ling, grabbed him linebacker-style around the waist, driving him away from his quarry. She shook a scolding finger in his face, then whipped out a dive slate and scribbled: POISON!

Dante squinted at the message, his vision darkening at the edges. He could see all the letters, but for the life of him, he couldn't put them together to read the word. What the young photographer didn't realize was that he was experiencing nitrogen narcosis — the rapture of the deep. Under deep-water pressure, the nitrogen in air dissolves in the bloodstream, producing an effect similar to drunkenness. In diving lingo, he was "narced."

THE DEEP

8

All Dante registered was that he was having a fine time, and here was Star, ruining it. The lionfish had gotten away, leaving Dante sweating from his efforts.

Who needs a rubber suit to dive in boiling water?

Before Star's horrified eyes, Dante unzipped his lightweight tropical skin suit and began to peel off the thin material. In his narced state, he had forgotten that the wet suit was not for warmth; it was for protection from the sting of coral and other venomous sea life.

She grabbed him and held on. He fought back, the upper half of the wet suit flapping from his waist.

That was when she saw the shark.

CHAPTER TWO

It was a bull shark, seven or eight feet long, although it looked even bigger through the lens of the water. It was not Clarence — the teen divers had already had a run-in with the eighteen-foot tiger shark of local legend. But Star was an expert diver, and she knew bulls could be aggressive. Especially if this one mistook their struggling for the thrashing of a wounded fish.

"Calm down!" she barked into her regulator, tasting salt water.

Dante was too impaired to heed the warning. His eyes were barely open, mere slits behind his mask.

The predator was only a few feet away, close enough for Star to see the peculiar remora fish clamped to its underside, attaching itself to feed on scraps of prey.

Star was torn. Should she swim away? But what about her partner? She was there for him, and he for her.

Onto the scene burst a blur of black rubber, a six-foot-five body formed by rigid discipline into the shape of a torpedo. It was Menasce Gérard, a hulking native dive guide with the unlikely nickname English. Propelled by the powerful kicks of his flippers, he swam into the shark's path. In a single motion, he pulled the dangling camera off Dante's arm, wheeled around, and brought it down with all his might on the bull's flat snout.

The shark reared up, shocked. Clearly, a bonk on the nose was the last thing it had expected. It turned abruptly and swam off, roiling the water. Out of the storm appeared a smaller fish — a foot long, with a round suction cup on its back. It was the remora, dislodged from its host during the commotion. It darted back and forth, searching in vain for the bull's pale underbelly. Finding nothing, it panicked and clamped onto Dante's bare chest.

That got Dante's attention. He cried out in shock, blowing a cloud of bubbles into English's face. He tried to pluck the remora from his skin, but the hold was too strong. Even the guide couldn't seem to yank the fish free.

English gave the signal to surface, but Dante was focused on his new tenant. "Get off me! Get off me!" He swallowed water, putting himself in a choking frenzy.

The guide took hold of Dante from behind, crossing his arms in an iron grip. Unable to reach his own B.C., he shot air into Dante's until they both began to rise. Star joined the shaky ascent.

They surfaced about twenty yards from the R/V *Hernando Cortés*, their dive boat. Symptoms of narcosis disappear as a diver rises, so Dante was no longer dazed. Now he was hysterical. "Pull it off! Pull it off!"

Doubting the boy could even swim in his frantic state, English towed him Red Cross–style to the *Cortés*. The other two teenage interns, Bobby Kaczinski and Adriana Ballantyne, hauled him onto the dive platform.

Adriana gawked at the fish fastened onto Dante. "What's *that*?"

English scrambled up beside them. "Remora!" he exclaimed, trying to work his hands under the creature's suction cup.

"You're hurting me!" cried Dante.

Star was last out of the water. She kicked off her flippers and approached Dante. She walked with a limp — the result of a mild case of cerebral palsy — although underwater the condition disappeared. Hefting her dripping air tank, she began smacking the remora with the flat bottom. Dante staggered backward, flopping down on the deck. "What are you trying to do, kill me?" he gasped.

"Silence, you silly child!" ordered English in his French Caribbean accent. This was not his first run-in with the four teens, and he was not in the mood to be understanding. "We do nothing, you complain! We do something, you complain louder!"

"But what if it's stuck on forever?"

"What's all the commotion?" Captain Braden Vanover peered down from the flying bridge. Spying the fish attached to Dante's chest, he exclaimed, "Oh, jeez!" and disappeared below.

He returned a moment later, carrying a bottle of Jamaican rum and a hypodermic syringe. He dipped the needle in the liquor, drew up some dark brown liquid, and injected it into the remora, just behind the gill slits.

The gray fish dropped to the deck, flipping wildly on the olive-painted planks. English expertly kicked it back into the sea.

Then he wheeled his furious attention on Dante. "You were maybe trying out for the *Sports Illustrated* swimsuit issue, monsieur? Why do you take off the wet suit at eighty feet?"

"He was narced," supplied Star.

"It wasn't my fault," Dante defended himself. "How was I supposed to know that crazy fish was going to stick on? It could happen to anybody."

"If it was not you, then it would not happen!" the guide seethed. "All of you — you attract the troubles like the giant magnet!" He turned to face Vanover. "I am finished with these American teenagers. I am not MTV, me! The next time they dive with you, you will find another guide!" He peeled off his dripping wet suit and stormed below.

"I'm Canadian," Kaz called after him. If English had heard, the big man gave no sign.

The four interns exchanged agonized looks. Their internship was a sham — a smokescreen for Tad Cutter's treasure hunting. Scuba trips with Captain Vanover and English were all that kept this summer from being a total bust. Now they were gone too.

"Well," the captain said slowly. "You've heard the bad news. Anybody ready for the good news?"

"We could sure use some," said Adriana.

"The office just radioed in. The PUSH team wrapped up their research a few days early. The next project doesn't start down there for another week. The station is yours if you want it."

CHAPTER THREE

The Poseidon Underwater Self-contained Habitat, or PUSH, was a subsea lab built right onto the Hidden Shoals proper, sixty-five feet beneath the waves. There, scientists called aquanauts could live and work for days at a time, spending almost every waking minute diving.

For Star, it was a dream come true. "The only problem with scuba is it's over too fast. But on PUSH, when your air runs low, you just swim to the station, switch tanks, and swim back out again. And there's no decompressing because you don't have to return to surface pressure. Home is right there on the reef."

"Home is an underwater sardine can," Dante said sourly.

"Even when you're not diving, it's still awesome," Star went on. "Because you're under sixty-five feet of water. Look out the window, and you're right in the thick of things."

"We'll be in the thick of things, all right," grumbled Dante. "Every time you crook your finger, you'll be picking somebody else's nose."

The four were in the cabin the two girls

shared, watching Adriana pack for their undersea sojourn. The girl gazed bleakly from the stacks of color-coordinated designer outfits to the tiny watertight bag about the size of a kindergartner's knapsack. Anything that wouldn't fit had to be left on dry land.

"This is impossible," she complained. "If I take the rust shorts, then I'm stuck with the matching sweatshirt. And it's so puffy, it fills the whole bag!"

"Rust?" repeated Dante. "Is that supposed to be a color?"

Adriana nodded. "It's between taupe and burnt sienna."

"Well, thanks for clearing that up," Dante said sarcastically. "Just pack any old thing. We're going to be so sick of looking at one another that you could wear a rabbit suit and nobody would notice."

"And bring your toothbrush," added Star. "We'll be breathing recycled air, but I doubt the CO_2 scrubbers can do anything about bad breath."

It was important not to forget anything. Once they had been at the station for half a day or so, a return to the surface meant seventeen hours in a decompression chamber.

As soon as their bags were packed, the four

THE DEEP

took advantage of their last chance to e-mail family and friends from Poseidon's computer lab. PUSH had computers linked by wireless telemetry to the outside world. But the connection was expensive, so there were strict rules against using it for personal correspondence.

Kaz replied to messages from his parents and Steven Allagash, his sports agent. Kaz was a hot prospect to make it as a professional hockey player. They called him the most promising young defenseman to come out of the Toronto area in twenty years.

That was *before*.

He sent just one more e-mail, to a boy named Drew Christiansen. The two were not friends. In fact, Kaz couldn't understand why Drew didn't consider him Public Enemy Number One after what had happened.

The Ontario Minor Hockey Association finals, game six. Kaz could still feel the contact of the body check as he drove Drew away from the net. It was a clean hit — even Drew agreed on that. A freak accident, according to the doctors. Trauma to the spinal column.

In that terrible instant, Drew Christiansen and Bobby Kaczinski were both out of hockey for good.

Drew had no choice in the matter. He would never walk again. And Kaz wanted nothing to do with a sport that could turn him into an instrument of destruction. That was why he had applied for the Poseidon internship. Diving in the Caribbean, it had seemed at the time, was the opposite of hockey in Canada.

He felt more than a little ridiculous e-mailing "How I Spent My Summer Vacation" to this stranger whose life he'd ruined.

But I'm not going to pretend it didn't happen —

"Hey, guys," called Adriana excitedly from another workstation. "I've got an answer from my uncle!"

Adriana's uncle Alfred Ballantyne was an antiquities expert. She had e-mailed him a photograph of an artifact Star had brought up from the shipwreck site — an elaborately carved whalebone hilt.

Adriana dropped her voice to a whisper as the others gathered around. They hadn't told anyone else about the artifact. If word of their find got back to Tad Cutter, they had no question that the treasure hunter would try to take it from them, just as he'd stolen their piece of eight, the Spanish silver coin. There was no way to be sure who they could trust at the institute. The only safe course was to trust no one.

Adriana pointed to the body of the message. "Right here."

. . . I don't think your artifact is the hilt of a sword or dagger, since there is no evidence of a guard or cross-piece. My best guess is that it is the handle of a walking stick, or perhaps even a whip (popular on ocean voyages for keeping both the crew and the rats in line).

I can't identify the stone because of the coral encrusting it, but I'm sure you noticed the letters JB carved just below there. These are the initials perhaps of the artisan, but more likely the owner. Above you'll see a design depicting a sprig of thistles. You'll recognize this as the symbol of the Stuarts, British monarchs who ruled in the seventeenth and early eighteenth centuries. Therefore, the item must have been crafted in England at that time. . . .

"Whoa," breathed Kaz. "That thing is one heavy-duty museum piece."

"And to think I've got it stashed in my underwear drawer," added Star.

"Yeah, but he doesn't tell us how much it's *worth*," put in Dante, who tended to view these artifacts in terms of dollars and cents. "Scroll down. Let's see what else he says."

"Oh, that's about the carving in English's window," Adriana told him. "I sent Uncle Alfie a picture of that too."

The native dive guide's cottage window displayed a large fragment of what once had been a huge carving of an eagle. It was apparently some kind of family heirloom. English refused to talk about it.

Adriana scrolled down.

. . . **Your other specimen presents somewhat more of a puzzle. One possible explanation for its European origin is that it may have broken off a ship. Old wooden vessels were festooned with elaborate sculptures, which their superstitious makers believed would ward off bad luck, evil spirits, hurricanes, fever, and pirates. The eagle may be of English style, so perhaps that's why your friend is called English. . . .**

THE DEEP

"Friend," snorted Kaz. "With friends like him, who needs Ming the Merciless?"

"Hi, team." Marina Kappas was working her way between the rows of computer desks toward them.

Instantly, Adriana closed her e-mail program. Marina was on Tad Cutter's crew of treasure hunters. On the surface, she was affable, outgoing, and seemed genuinely concerned about the teens' well-being. She was also flat-out gorgeous, which scored a lot of points with Kaz and Dante. It had far less effect on the girls. And all four had to bear in mind that, beautiful or not, friendly or not, as Cutter's colleague, she was on the other team.

"I hear they've stolen you away for a few days at PUSH," Marina went on. "We'll miss you guys."

"I can tell," Star said sarcastically. "There's something about getting up at four in the morning to take off without us that shows you really care."

Cutter and company had been avoiding their interns since day one.

Marina shrugged. "Workaholics. Tad and Chris are crazy when they're on a project. Hey, you're going to love PUSH. Not much elbow room, but really fascinating."

The four exchanged a meaningful glance. Marina Kappas didn't care if they were fascinated or not. She just wanted them down on the station, out of the way, leaving her team free to continue the search for sunken treasure — with no prying eyes to watch them.

CHAPTER FOUR

The bow of the R/V *Francisco Pizarro* cleaved the light chop of an otherwise flawless Caribbean. It was the interns' first ride with Captain Janet Torrington, whose job it was to deliver them to PUSH for a five-day stay.

The captain was telling them about Dr. Igor Ocasek, the scientist who would be sharing the small station with them.

"The thing about Iggy is that he's a genius, which means half the time he seems as dumb as a box of rocks. When his mind is on a problem, you can be three inches in front of his nose, screaming your lungs out, and he has no idea you're even there."

"What is he studying?" asked Adriana.

Torrington shrugged. "His specialty is mollusks, but right now I'd have to say he's a Doctor of Tinkering."

"Tinkering?" Kaz echoed.

"You know, fiddling with stuff. Retooling, refitting, rewiring. He can improve anything. Iggy designed a better *paper clip* last year, if you can believe it. Superior ergonomics, whatever

DIVE

that is. It's up in Washington now, patent pending."

As they approached the Hidden Shoals, Torrington slowed to a crawl, and the *Pizarro* began to pick her way gingerly through a minefield of marker buoys. These indicated coral heads towering so close to the surface that they presented a hazard to shipping. It was no joke. A living reef concealed a limestone core strong enough to rip open the hull of a boat.

Kaz pointed at the outline of another vessel undulating in the heat shimmer on the horizon. "Isn't that the *Ponce de León*?" Tad Cutter's boat.

Dante frowned at the silhouette. "I thought he was spending all his time over the wreck site."

"That *is* the wreck site!" Star exclaimed. "I wonder how far away we'll be."

As if on cue, Captain Torrington cut power as the *Pizarro* bumped up alongside the PUSH life-support buoy. She sprang to the gunwale and tied on.

"Last stop, folks. Your home away from home."

The four interns began the process of pulling on their lightweight wet suits.

"This couldn't have worked out better," Star said in a low voice. "It's our perfect chance to check out the wreck site on our own."

THE DEEP

Dante worked the tight arm strap of his Nikonos past his elbow. "I don't know, Star. That looks like a half-mile swim from here. Maybe you can make it, but we can't — not there and back again."

Star shrugged into her compressed air tank. "Then I'll go myself."

Adriana stared at her. "Alone?" The buddy system was practically carved in stone for divers.

"Cutter and his crew could be pulling millions of dollars' worth of stuff out of that wreck, and we'd never know the difference," Star argued. "This is the only way we'll find out for sure." She flipped down her mask. "Let's go."

With their watertight bags tethered to their B.C. vests, the four climbed down to the dive platform, stepped into their flippers, and jumped down to the waves.

Captain Torrington waved. "See you next week. Tell Iggy I said hi."

Still on the surface, Star switched her underwater watch to compass mode and took a careful reading of the *Ponce de León*. Just past east-northeast.

They valved air from their vests and descended, slipping easily through the chop. The instant Star was underwater, she felt her disability vanish. Down here, there was no weakness on the left side — or any side. This was the medium that was meant for Star Ling. She was comfortable; she was graceful; she was home.

It wasn't a recreational dive. In fact, all they were supposed to do was follow the buoy's umbilical lines directly down to PUSH.

Star passed through a shimmering cloud of blue-and-white-striped grunts. She was already well ahead of the others. She was used to waiting for them. Kaz, Dante, and Adriana were inexperienced divers. It had baffled the interns at first — why pick a bunch of beginners for a prestigious internship? Now they understood perfectly. Tad Cutter had been betting that novices wouldn't discover his secret plans. He'd also been convinced that Star's disability would keep her from getting in his way.

Better luck next time, Tad, old pal.

As she passed a hovering sea horse, the sunlight from above provided an X ray of its pale brown translucent body. *She's pregnant!* thought Star, and then quickly corrected herself. *He's pregnant.* In a rare reversal of nature, *male* sea horses carried the young.

PUSH looked like a giant car engine on the ocean floor. At the center was the station's main living space — a steel tube ten feet wide and fifty feet long. Star floated beside an underwater rack of compressed air tanks as the others joined her.

Since the station's underbelly was mirrored, the entrance seemed like a square hole in the middle of the ocean, a magical portal to dry land sixty-five feet beneath the waves. The feeling of hoisting herself through the opening into the pressurized air was unreal.

A short metal ladder led up to the wet porch. There, the interns shrugged out of their gear.

"Check it out!" Star pointed to a rack of six diver propulsion vehicles, or DPVs. The scooters looked a lot like bombs. In reality, their "tails" were protective housing for the propellers that moved them through the water. "Transportation to the wreck site."

The four unpacked their watertight luggage — nothing wet was allowed past the hatchway that led to PUSH's living area. They each carried an armload of belongings as they passed barefoot through the pressure hatch into the entry lock.

A rapid series of pops, like machine-gun fire, resounded in the confined space. Kaz, who led the way, was pelted by a barrage of hot, stinging projectiles.

He gawked. Popcorn littered the dark industrial carpet. At the center of the chamber knelt a young man with long flyaway hair. He held a blowtorch under an enormous conch shell that was overflowing with popped kernels.

Spying them, he quickly shut off the blowtorch. "Sorry about that. Welcome to PUSH. I'm Iggy Ocasek." Unable to shake hands in greeting, he held out the shell. "Hungry?"

"No thanks." Kaz performed the introductions. "Kaz, Star, Adriana, Dante." The latter two were on their hands and knees gathering up clothing dropped during the snack attack.

"This isn't what it looks like," Dr. Ocasek explained, setting shell and torch on a stainless steel counter. "Poseidon is about to authorize a major study of how mollusk shells conduct heat at depth. I figured, I've got mollusks, I've got heat, I've got depth, I've got — "

"Popcorn?" finished Adriana.

"You learn to improvise down here," the scientist admitted. "And you've got to admit that the shell conducted heat beautifully."

While Dr. Ocasek vacuumed up the popcorn with a handheld portable vacuum, the four interns explored their surroundings. The habitat was laid out like the cabin of a commuter jet. A narrow hallway stretched from end to end, flanked by looming steel walls of switches, dials, and readouts. Bare bulbs provided harsh, unyielding light. There were occasional comforts of

THE DEEP

home — a microscopic bathroom ringed by a flimsy privacy curtain, a small refrigerator/ freezer, a microwave, a built-in dining booth to seat six.

"Six *hobbits*," put in Dante.

At the far end of the station, bunks were stacked three high on either side of the corridor. It wasn't difficult to spot Dr. Ocasek's berth on the bottom left. It was unmade, with tools, a roll of electrician's tape, bits of cable, and a soldering gun scattered around the sheets. Beside it, the metal wall plate was gone. Through the opening, an electric blanket had been hardwired into the guts of the habitat.

"I guess it gets chilly at night," Star observed dryly.

"That guy's nuts," said Dante with conviction. "If he short-circuits the station, no more air pumps, and we all suffocate."

"He's just eccentric, that's all," soothed Kaz.

"Maybe so, but I'm sleeping with my scuba tank."

Star laughed. "Suit yourself. Come on, let's go find a shipwreck."

CHAPTER FIVE

The double-tank setup was awkward and heavy, and Adriana struggled to get used to its bulk. The extra air supply made sense, though. Since they didn't have to worry about decompressing back to the surface, PUSH aquanauts could dive for hours at a time.

As Dr. Ocasek swam around to help get the others outfitted with extra air cylinders from the underwater rack, a four-foot moray eel followed him like an adoring puppy. Every now and then, the scientist would reach into his dive pouch and toss the creature a lump of food.

"Peanut butter sandwich," he explained into his regulator.

Peanut butter was the staple on the station. Adriana had checked the tiny pantry and found fourteen jars of the stuff, and precious little else.

That's how you know when it's time to leave PUSH, she thought to herself. *When your tongue is permanently stuck to the roof of your mouth.*

At last, all was ready, and the four yanked the trigger handles of their DPVs. The propellers whirred, pulling them forward. As Adriana glided silkily through the water, her awkwardness fell away. It wasn't the speed that astonished her. In fact, she was only traveling a few miles per hour. No, what amazed Adriana was the total ease with which she moved over the coral and sponge formations of the reef. Diving had never been second nature for her, like it was for Star.

Hanging on to the handles of the scooter, she fell into line behind Star, who navigated by the compass on her dive watch. A pair of eagle rays raced her for a while before veering off, wings undulating. Even her breathing was easier — slow, natural breaths instead of her usual gasping sucks on the regulator. Kaz flashed her thumbs-up. Even Dante was grinning. This was the only way to travel.

She felt like a tourist, taking in the scenery and enjoying the ride. Freed from the mechanics of scuba, she vibrated with nervous anticipation. A seventeenth-century shipwreck!

Her brow clouded a little. After two straight summers working with her uncle at the British Museum, the job had fallen through this year. Alfred Ballantyne could only bring one assistant to Syria on his archaeological dig. He had chosen Adriana's brother, Payton. The Poseidon internship had been almost a consolation prize.

But a three-hundred-year-old wreck! That beat

a Middle Eastern dig any day — or at least it would have if it hadn't been for Cutter and the team of treasure hunters.

By the time she noticed the roar, she realized she'd been hearing it for a while already. She peered past Star, trying to identify the source of the noise. But up ahead the water had become murky, almost opaque.

They had seen this effect before. Something was kicking up tons of mud and silt, churning the clear blue Caribbean into a turbulent blind tunnel of swirling brown.

An explosion? Cutter had done this before — dynamiting the reef to get at what was underneath the coral.

But no. The sound was steady, not a sudden blast. And it was increasing in volume. Whatever the source of the roar, it was getting closer.

And then, directly ahead, an unseen power grabbed hold of Star and flung her contemptuously aside.

Adriana froze as she tried to wrap her mind around what had happened. By the time she could react, the irresistible force had pounced on her.

The ocean itself was moving, a deep-water riptide. With overwhelming strength, it hurled her — up, down, sideways? It was impossible to tell.

Rocks and chunks of flotsam battered her, caught up in the whirlpool. The mask was torn from her face as she whipped violently around. All sensation ceased to be. There was only pure motion, pure speed.

When she struck the coral, the collision sucked the wind out of her and knocked the regulator from her mouth. She lost her grip on the DPV. The scooter fell away, its auto-shutoff cutting power. Everything went dark.

Am I dead?

Her next gasping breath drew in a lungful of water. The choking was violent, desperate.

No — alive — The thoughts were fragments, half formed, rattling around the darkness of her mind. *Alive — and drowning —*

With effort, she forced her eyes open against the sting of salt water. She flailed for her mouthpiece, finding it at last and biting down hard. The rush of air brought her back to herself. Her body ached and her eyes hurt like crazy.

Can't close them! Have to see!

Dante was taking the brunt of it now. Fins windmilling wildly, he spun out of control, striking a mound of brain coral. Was he okay? Where was Kaz? And what had happened to Star?

All at once, the roar ceased. As the silt storm began to resolve itself, Adriana could just make out a silhouette standing near the source of the disturbance.

Too big to be Star . . . Kaz?

She reached up to wave, but an iron grip held her arm in place. Strong hands pulled her behind the stout base of a coral head. There crouched Kaz and Star.

Then who is the silhouette?

Star scribbled the answer on her dive slate: REARDON.

Adriana squinted. She could make out the stocky diver's beard below his mask. Chris Reardon, Cutter's other partner. The third treasure hunter wielded what looked like an enormous hose, a foot thick or more. Was that what had tossed the interns around like wisps of algae?

Her eyes were killing her. She had to find her mask! Wincing with pain, she searched the bottom. Where had it fallen? And then she spotted it, nestled in a growth of pink anemones.

Reardon hit a switch, and the roar returned. In less than a second, the mask disappeared in the blizzard of silt. Adriana squeezed her eyes shut in an attempt to protect them from the swirling particles that were everywhere in the water.

She was stuck. They were all stuck.

CHAPTER SIX

Aboard the R/V *Ponce de León*, the noise was earsplitting, far louder than it was underwater.

The device was known as an airlift, but Cutter and his team called it Diplodocus. The long, thick hose stretching over the gunwale of their boat into the water resembled a sauropod dinosaur, its long neck drooping in a lazy arc as it drank from some Jurassic lagoon.

The contraption was basically a souped-up vacuum cleaner, strong enough to suck chunks of coral all the way from the ocean bottom. It was definitely not a toy. It had the power to break up limestone, or to rip a person's arm clean off. Handling the airlift's nozzle was no easy task. Reardon had to dive with weighted boots and a sixty-pound lead belt to avoid being tossed about at the end of the massive hose.

Their work was as exhausting as it was boring, but this was the only way to excavate a shipwreck long buried in a living reef: First, use Diplodocus as a blower in order to blast the weakened coral to bits, kicking up all the mud and artifacts trapped underneath. Then, vac-

DIVE

uum up the debris and search for something of value.

That was what Cutter and Marina were doing. The backwash from the airlift was deposited into a huge wire-mesh basket that floated off the *Ponce de León*'s stern. Load by load, the two treasure hunters winched the tons of broken coral on deck, combing painstakingly through it, breaking up larger chunks with hammers.

So far, they had recovered a great deal of items in this way — ceramic cups, bowls, and plates, glass bottles, brass buttons and medallions, rusted metal nails, hinges, pulleys, buckles, musket shot, and cannonballs. Old ballast stones littered the deck of the research vessel. An anchor and the coral-encrusted barrels of two cannons lay out of sight in the ship's hold. They had found every sort of artifact — with one exception.

"Where's the treasure?" roared Cutter, tapping at a lump of coral with half a saucer encased in it. "We didn't go through all this for a boatload of broken dishes!"

"The kids found a piece of eight," Marina pointed out, tossing a ball of grapeshot on top of a pile of the stuff.

"Yeah, one coin out of a king's ransom," Cutter said disgustedly. "*Nuestra Señora de la Luz* was packed with silver and gold. That fleet carried the wealth of Asia and South America for an entire year! Where is it?"

Marina frowned. "Can we be *sure* this is *Nuestra Señora de la Luz*?"

"It has to be. Every knickknack we pull up is Spanish in origin. There was only one galleon lost off Saint-Luc in the mid-seventeenth century. Most of the treasure fleets took the northern route, via Havana and the Florida Straits." He sighed. "I guess we'll just have to dig harder."

He signaled Bill Hamilton, captain of the *Ponce de León*, who activated the winch. The small crane hoisted the basket up off its raft, and another load of debris hit the deck between the two treasure hunters.

Cutter stared. Buried amid the coral fragments was a dive mask.

"Chris!" Marina shouted.

They rushed to the gunwale and peered below. Reardon wasn't technically scuba diving. He was breathing through a long hose connected to a Brownie compressor that floated beside the boat. Marina grabbed the safety line and gave two sharp tugs, the UP signal.

They waited — a breathless wait.

Marina looked nervous. "Decomp?"

Reardon had been on the bottom at sixty-five feet for nearly an hour — long enough to start thinking about decompression. Maybe he had paused during his ascent.

The alternative was too awful to think about: If he had somehow gotten his head caught in the airlift's nozzle . . .

And then Reardon broke the surface with a splash. His swimming was awkward because of his heavy belt and boots, but he managed to struggle to the Brownie.

"What's the problem?" he called.

Seeing the mask on their partner's face, Cutter and Marina exchanged a confused glance.

Marina cupped her hands to her mouth. "Did you see anything down there?"

"Are you kidding?" came the reply. "When that monster's on, I can barely see my hands in front of my face."

Cutter turned to Marina. "This is a popular dive spot. That mask could have been there for years."

She examined the faceplate, molded plastic, and rubber headband. There wasn't a speck of coral, algae, or anemone growth anywhere.

"Yeah, probably," she said. But she didn't sound convinced.

After some frantic searching, the divers were able to locate their DPVs in the murky water. Adriana never found her mask.

It was a tense ride back to the station. The interns barely noticed the spectacular colors of the reef, or the multitudes of creatures that darted around, agitated by the airlift's tempest. All thoughts were riveted to their near miss. No serious injuries, and Reardon hadn't seen them. But it had been close. Too close.

Star's eyes never left the glowing dial of the compass on her dive watch. She led the way until she reached one of the fixed navigation lines that fanned out from PUSH. There they turned left and followed the white rope until the familiar shape of the habitat appeared out of the blue.

Dante was last up the ladder, but he was already babbling excitedly the instant his mouth cleared the water in the wet porch. "Man, what hit us, an underwater tornado?"

He was interrupted by a low, muffled banging.

Adriana started. "What was that?"

But there was the sound again, like someone knocking on glass.

Dante peered out the viewing port.

"Who are you looking for?" Star asked in an amused tone. "The Avon lady?"

And then a loud, tinny amplified voice blared, *"No! Over here!"*

The four interns jumped. Dr. Ocasek peered

out at them from the round window of the station's decompression chamber.

"Sorry to startle you," the scientist chuckled through the intercom. "I know you weren't expecting to find me in here. I have to rush topside."

In PUSH language, rushing meant getting there seventeen hours later. It took that long for the chamber to bring an aquanaut back to surface pressure without risk of the bends — decompression sickness. The interns would have to go through the same treatment when their stay was over.

"I thought you were here for another week," Kaz said.

"It's kind of an emergency," Dr. Ocasek admitted. "A small explosion in my part of the lab up there. I can't understand it. My experiments hardly ever explode."

"Is it safe for us to stay here on our own?" Dante asked uneasily.

"Oh, they're sending someone else down. I assured them that you kids are totally independent. But you know what a worrywart Geoffrey can be."

"Right," said Kaz. They were certain that Dr. Geoffrey Gallagher couldn't have cared less about the four of them. If Poseidon's director was worried, it was over the bad publicity that would fall on the institute if anything happened to four teenagers on their guest staff. That kind of black eye might even shut down production of the documentary film that was going to make him the next Jacques Cousteau.

They shrugged out of their gear and filed through the pressure hatch into the station proper.

"You've got to be more careful," Star admonished Dante. "You almost spilled the beans in front of Iggy back there."

Kaz was shocked. "You think *Iggy's* in with Cutter and his people?"

"Of course not," Star replied. "But if we keep quiet, there's less chance of word getting back to Cutter that we're onto him. For all we know, Iggy is Poseidon's number one blabbermouth. We don't want him spreading it around that Reardon's down on the reef with something that nearly blew us up."

"I think that thing was an airlift," Adriana said. "Some of the underwater archaeologists at the British Museum use them, but only as a last resort. They're so strong that they sometimes smash more artifacts than they collect."

"They smash innocent by-swimmers too," Dante added.

"We were lucky," Adriana said solemnly.

"How do you figure that?" asked Kaz.

"An airlift works like a vacuum cleaner. We got to Reardon when it was blowing *out*, breaking up debris. If we'd come along when the nozzle was set to suck, somebody could have gotten killed."

"That's our treasure they're vacuuming," Dante complained bitterly. "If they get rich off *our* discovery — "

"They won't," Star promised. "But first we'd better see exactly what they've found over there."

"What are we going to do?" challenged Kaz. "Swim up and tell Reardon we're stealing back our shipwreck?"

"No," replied Star, "we wait till he goes home and *then* steal it back."

"But you know Cutter's schedule," Dante protested. "He's on that reef from the crack of dawn till after dark. The only time to avoid him would be the middle of the —"

The others stared at Star in dismay. Was she suggesting that they navigate all the way to the excavation and back again in the inky blackness of underwater night?

She looked at them pityingly. "They're called lights, guys. Maybe you've heard of them." A broad grin split her delicate features. "And just wait till you get a load of the ocean at night."

CHAPTER SEVEN

Kaz peered nervously down at the black water at the bottom of the hatch. He was afraid, no question about it. Not of the usual night hazards — becoming lost or disoriented. Or torch failure, which could strand a diver in a silent world of infinite dark.

No, Kaz's fear stemmed directly from the object of his greatest childhood interest and obsession: sharks.

Sharks are night feeders. It was in every single volume of an entire home library dedicated to the sea predators. Did that mean nocturnal divers were in any extra danger? Even the experts weren't sure.

Kaz had never truly understood his lifelong fascination with sharks until he'd come face to face with them in the waters of the Hidden Shoals. That had cleared it all up: He was scared to death of them.

Most of the local sharks were nurse and reef sharks three or four feet long — pretty harmless, if you didn't make them mad. But Kaz knew that larger, more aggressive cousins — bulls, ham-

DIVE

merheads, makos — also prowled these waters. And somewhere lurked Clarence, the eighteen-foot monster tiger shark with a gullet large enough to swallow a filing cabinet whole.

Suppressing his unease, Kaz started down the ladder. "I'll go first," he mumbled, then bit his mouthpiece and let the water swallow him up.

The headlamp in his dive hood created a zone of illumination around him, a funnel-shaped cocoon of light in the great dark sea. He finned away from the station's bulk, adjusting his buoyancy with the B.C. valve. The reef's rush hour was over. But he soon realized that the water was just as crowded with different, smaller creatures. The ocean was alive with millions of undulating blue larvae, each one just a few millimeters long. They hung there, absolutely defenseless, as they were attacked by the thousands by tiny, round, tentacled predators —

Polyps! Kaz thought in sudden understanding. *At night, coral polyps dislodge from the reef and go hunting!* He was witnessing the very bottom of a food chain that extended all the way to Clarence, wherever he was.

Far away, I hope.

The other interns floated around him now, taking in the night scene. Following Star's lead, they switched off their headlamps. The ocean seemed pitch-black at first, yet as Kaz's eyes adjusted, he began to see the glow of the moon, penetrating through sixty-five feet of water. Light and color shone all around them from the bodies of fish. It was bioluminescence — the emission of light from living creatures. Like a large moving mushroom, a jellyfish glowed pale pink as it pulsed by. Even the plankton was bioluminescent, causing the water itself to sparkle like glitter makeup.

They switched their headlamps back on, and Star led the way to the wreck site, navigating by the compass on her watch. It gave Kaz a giddy feeling of power to outrace the fish, many of which appeared to be asleep. Some hung motionless in the water; others had attached themselves to kelp and sea fans. There were even a few "sleepwalkers."

Sleep-swimmers, Kaz corrected himself.

The wreck site was difficult to find. They would have missed it completely if the water hadn't still been a little cloudy from the use of the airlift hours earlier. With their DPVs set on low, they circled the area, spiraling gradually inward, until at last Dante's sharp eyes fell on the coral ditch that was Cutter's excavation.

Adriana emptied her B.C. to lessen her buoyancy. Setting down her scooter, she planted herself on her knees on the bottom and began to sift through the limestone rubble. She worked alone for a few moments while the others hung back, uncertain what to do. Then, noticing their inactivity, she gestured impatiently for them to join her.

Kaz settled himself beside her and began to sort debris. The operation reminded him of the time he was eight when the phone company had busted up the Kaczinski driveway to repair a broken wire. The neighborhood kids had spent days "mining" the blocks of blacktop. It had been a good time, made doubly precious to Kaz by the fact that he was constantly being whisked off to some hockey practice while everybody else had fun.

But here — two thousand miles, sixty-five vertical feet, and two atmospheres of pressure from his home in Toronto — there was an immediacy, a truth to this moment. This was a real shipwreck, pursued by real treasure hunters. And the treasure, if it was there, would be worth real money — millions, probably.

Enough to change our lives forever.

It was theirs for the taking — or losing, if they stood by and let Cutter's people have their way. He dug faster.

Gold fever. He remembered the term from a social studies unit on the Klondike gold rush. He could feel himself coming down with the disease.

THE DEEP

The oppressive click and hiss of his own breathing was amplified by the scuba gear. It was accelerating, and so was his heartbeat. The moment when he would push aside a block of coral to reveal gleaming treasure underneath seemed so close he could almost taste it. And the compulsion to keep digging overpowered everything, even fatigue.

He could see it in the urgent actions of his fellow divers as well. It was especially obvious in Dante's intense, almost crazed eyes, magnified by the prescription lens of his mask.

They worked tirelessly, moving blocks that would have been far too heavy to handle on land. The increased effort ate up their air supplies, and soon it was time to switch to the backup tanks.

Kaz hurriedly snapped the hose back into place. His first breath drew a mouthful of burning salt water into his lungs. Choking, he fumbled with the connection, desperate to restore the flow of air. He finally got it right, but each convulsive hack drew in more water, causing a chain reaction of coughing.

Star grabbed him by the shoulders. "Are you all right?" she shouted into her mouthpiece.

Kaz tried to signal okay with his thumb and forefinger, but he could not get his breathing back under control. With effort, he narrowed his focus to the bowl-shaped debris field below them. The less he thought about the constant tickle in his throat, the less he was likely to cough. But the search was becoming frustrating. There was nothing here but a pile of rocks.

He frowned. This couldn't be right. The shattered coral was jagged, random. But these rocks were round, and mostly smooth, like quarry stones. What were they doing at the bottom of the Caribbean?

He cast a perplexed look at Adriana. It was hard to read the expression behind her mask, but her eyes were alight with excitement. She pulled her dive slate from the pocket of her vest and wrote: BALLAST.

Of course! She had told them about this. Old wooden ships carried tons of ballast rocks to prevent them from keeling over in rough seas.

This is it! The ship itself, locked in coral for more than three hundred years!

Then, as if his realization had opened the floodgates, the artifacts began to come. First, Star pulled out what looked like a lump on a stick. Upon closer inspection, it was a pewter spoon, its bone handle imprisoned in coral. Next, Dante's sharp eyes fell on a fragment of a dinner plate. A brass crucifix was Adriana's first find, followed by a handful of lead musket balls. More cutlery followed — they stuffed dozens of spoons and knives in their mesh dive bags. Dante pulled out another plate, this one intact except for a small wedge-shaped nick in the edging. Star came up with a small glass bottle in perfect condition.

Dante scribbled TREASURE?! on his slate. Adriana shook her head impatiently, digging with both gloved hands. Her face glowed with purpose.

Kaz latched onto a round coral fragment and brought it into the beam of his headlamp. The light flickered, then stabilized, giving him his first good look at the object before him.

A scream was torn from his throat, dispatching a cloud of bubbles to the surface.

There, partially encased in coral, was a human skull.

The skull slipped from his grip and settled back on the shattered reef. The others gawked in revulsion.

Calm down, Kaz told himself. *People die in shipwrecks. You know that. This is no great shock.*

But it was a shock. He was here to dive, not to come face-to-face with death.

It happened three hundred years ago! This is

no different from the mummy exhibit at the museum!

Star was more concerned about Kaz's flickering headlamp. Equipment failure could be even more devastating on a night dive. She checked her air supply. The gauge read 1600 psi, but the others were inexperienced divers, and probably had less. It was a good idea to head home.

Their bags full of artifacts, they returned to their scooters for the ride back to PUSH. Unlike the trip over, Kaz barely noticed the nocturnal life of the reef that was all around him. The horror-movie image of the skull hung before him like a totem of doom. How must it have felt to drown in these waters? Especially for a European sailor, so far from anything familiar?

We look at that wreck as an underwater ATM, he thought. *But it's also a mass grave.*

He felt the weight of the items in his goody bag tethered to his belt. Stealing from the dead. Well, not exactly. Nobody from that long-lost ship could have any use for this stuff now. But it didn't feel right.

Dr. Ocasek was still shut away in the decompression chamber, so it was pretty easy for the interns to smuggle their dive bags into the main lock. Adriana spread a towel over the stainless steel counter, and they placed their dripping artifacts across it.

Kaz stared intently at the coral-encrusted objects as if expecting some hidden discovery to burst upon him like a sunrise. Then he turned to Adriana. "Am I excited about this?"

"Of course," she replied with a frown. "All this stuff is consistent with the seventeenth century. The cutlery handles are made of bone or wood. And the workmanship looks a lot like things I've seen at the museum from the same time period."

"But you're not smiling," Star pointed out.

"It's *Spanish*." She pointed. "Crucifixes, Catholic religious medallions. See that helmet? Only Spain used that design — there were soldiers on the galleons, separate from the crew. The seamen couldn't fight, and the soldiers couldn't sail."

"Then it's definite!" cried Dante. "That's a real treasure ship! I just hope Cutter hasn't already boosted all the money."

"But the JB hilt is from England," Adriana reminded him. "My uncle identified it, and he's an antiquities expert. What was it doing on a Spanish galleon?"

Kaz shrugged. "Some Spanish guy bought an English walking stick. Or a whip, or whatever that handle is from."

"Or he could have stolen it," added Star.

"Maybe," Adriana admitted grudgingly. "But in those days you couldn't just go on the Internet and order stuff from around the world. And Spanish colonials were barred from buying foreign goods. An English artifact on a Spanish ship — I don't know. It sounds kind of fishy to me. There's something here we're not seeing. . . ."

30 August 1665

The settlement of Portobelo was ablaze. The bodies of its soldiers and citizens lay strewn about its ruined streets.

Samuel wandered through the bloody chaos, the blade of his sword striking sparks as he dragged it across the cobblestones. He did not have the strength to heft it, and certainly not the will. Samuel Higgins had been kidnapped from his family at the age of six, and had lived a life of privation and torment. Yet this was the lowest he had ever sunk in misery. He had not known the true mission of the Griffin *when he had signed on. Even upon learning the truth, he could never have imagined this frenzied rampage of torture and murder.*

Sick at heart, he walked away from the mayhem and started back to the beach. He had no definite plan. Perhaps he would sit on the sand and wait for this nightmare to be over. But he had not ruled out walking straight into the sea until the blue water swallowed him forever.

DIVE

And then his back exploded with pain, and he fell to the street, waiting for death. Surely, this was a musket ball that had struck him down. He turned, expecting to see a Spanish soldier reloading his weapon. Instead, it was the tall figure of Captain James Blade, furling the leather of his whip. Set in the handle, an emerald the size of a robin's egg gleamed cruelly in the sun.

"Going somewhere, boy?"

The true extent of his predicament brought Samuel out of his daze. Walking away in the middle of a battle was desertion — a hanging offense.

"Captain," he said beseechingly, "what use have you for me in this fight — a boy who cannot even lift his sword?"

"I'll kill you myself if you turn your back on your duty again!" Blade threatened. He reached down, grabbed a handful of Samuel's unruly brown hair, and drew the boy to his feet. "These foul maggots call you Lucky. Be they right or be they wrong, they take heart when they see you. And you will be seen!"

So Samuel dragged himself and his sword back to the battle.

Musket fire was heard in the alleyway behind the merchants' houses. A lead ball ripped into the stone wall of the church, missing Samuel by inches. Terri-

fied, he ran around the corner of the building and stopped short. There in front of him stood a captain of the Spanish garrison.

The officer reared back a double-edged broadsword, preparing to deliver a blow that would slice the cabin boy in half. Samuel raised his own sword in a feeble attempt to ward off the attack. He closed his eyes, waiting for it all to end.

Suddenly, distant drums resounded through the burning town, beating out the cease-fire. It was the garrison at Santiago, signaling the Spanish surrender.

Portobelo was won.

And young Samuel Higgins was still lucky.

CHAPTER EIGHT

Breakfast the next day was powdered milk and peanut butter on toast. After passing a serving through the airlock to Dr. Ocasek in the chamber, the interns suited up and headed back to the wreck site.

This time, they were careful to maintain a safe distance. As soon as the water turned murky and they could hear the airlift's roar, they retreated to a hiding place behind a coral ridge. There they waited, observing nothing but swirling clouds of silt until their air ran low.

Back at PUSH, the four found Dr. Ocasek out of decompression and all packed up for his return to the surface. "I just talked to topside," he told them. "Jennifer Delal will be coming down in a couple of hours. She's collecting algae samples from the reef."

"We got you a going-away present," said Star. From her mesh bag, she pulled an enormous conch shell nearly two feet long.

"Something to make popcorn in," Kaz supplied. "Just in case you get hungry topside."

The scientist was impressed. "Wow, that's a beauty! I'm going to miss you guys."

They watched through the viewing port as he exited the wet porch. The shell under his arm was larger than the waterproof bag that held all his belongings from a two-week stay. He tossed one final piece of sandwich to his "pet" moray, and disappeared up the tether line. A boat waited at the PUSH life-support buoy to whisk him off to deal with the wreckage of his workspace and his exploded experiments.

On the station, the time dragged. Sick of peanut butter, they tried to make a freeze-dried beef Stroganoff dinner from the pantry. But Kaz forgot to add water before heating. Gray smoke billowed from the microwave, setting off the top-side monitoring sensors.

"Don't worry," came the amused voice of the technician over the emergency wall speaker. "The habitat has air scrubbers that'll take out the smoke automatically. Just don't cook any more duck à l'orange, okay?"

"It was beef Stroganoff," Kaz admitted.

"Listen, nobody comes to PUSH for the fine cuisine," the man assured them. "Just sit tight until Dr. Delal gets there, got it?" He severed the connection.

"What about fish?" asked Dante. "That's

food, right? We're choking on peanut butter, and right outside our window is the ultimate seafood buffet."

Star laughed in his face. "Like you could cut open a fish without fainting."

"I did once," Adriana informed them. "Actually, it was at a resort, so the staff did all the gutting and cleaning. But I watched."

They settled in for a long wait on the cramped station. The water outside the viewing ports darkened from blue to black as night fell. There was still no sign of Dr. Delal.

Adriana sprang to her feet. "I'll call topside."

Star grabbed her arm. "They'll just order us to stay put again."

"Which is exactly what we're doing," agreed Kaz. "So what's the problem?"

"She probably just decided to hold off until morning, and they forgot to tell us," said Star. "Which means we'll sit here all night and lose our only chance to check out the wreck site when Cutter isn't there."

Dante stared at her. "You mean a night dive? Now? When we're all alone?"

"You think some scientist could help us if we ran into Clarence out there?" Kaz said.

"Is that supposed to make me feel better?" Dante demanded.

Star paced the narrow aisle, her limp exaggerated by the cramped quarters. "We'll give it till midnight," she decided. "Then we dive — Dr. Delal or no Dr. Delal."

At eleven-fifty-five, with no sign of the scientist, they dressed out and shrugged into the awkward double-tank setups.

The fifteen-minute half-mile ride to the wreck site was becoming familiar, Adriana reflected as she clung to the handles of the DPV. There was the coral head that reminded her of the Eiffel Tower, and the colony of tentacled anemones that resembled a field of powder-blue flowers. A little farther along, her headlamp illuminated the "lobster sponge," a titanic red sponge that was used as a hiding place by several clawless Caribbean lobsters.

I'm starting to recognize the fish too. The thought seemed crazy. But no — there was the barracuda that was missing the top half of its crescent tail. It was exciting, almost like running into an old friend.

I wonder if he knows us too — "Hey, it's those losers on the dive scooters. Who taught them how to swim?"

She became all business when they reached the wreck site. She worked tirelessly, stuffing her bag until it was bursting with coral-encrusted artifacts. The passion of her own efforts didn't surprise her. She loved this stuff. But she was amazed at the enthusiasm the others put into the job. It was backbreaking work, even underwater, where the blocks of limestone weighed much less than on dry land. At such a level of exertion, a diver sucked air at double speed, and soon Star was tapping her on the shoulder. Their backup tanks were down to half full. It was time to return to PUSH.

The trip home was a pleasantly exhausted one. Their DPVs worked a little slower from the weight of bags jam-packed with artifacts.

As she glided through the black water in her cone of light, her mind toyed lazily with the puzzle of the shipwreck. A Spanish vessel, almost certainly. Maybe even one of the fabled treasure galleons — the time period seemed about right. But where was the treasure? Surely Cutter couldn't have it all. That much silver and gold would sink the *Ponce de León*. And how did the bone handle fit in?

Maybe I'm making a mountain out of a molehill. She knew, for example, that English cannons were common on foreign ships. Was it really so weird that a Spaniard had acquired an item that had once belonged to an Englishman with the initials JB?

Something was wrong. Up ahead, she could see Star turning around. That was when Adriana realized that she had noticed none of the usual landmarks on the return trip. She checked her dive watch. They had been on the move for twenty minutes, maybe more. They should have reached the habitat by now.

With a feeling approaching fright, she realized they were lost.

CHAPTER NINE

Frantically, Adriana ransacked her mind for any clue as to where they had veered off course. Somehow, they must have skirted the circle of navigation lines that stretched out from PUSH like the spokes of a wheel. But how far back? And in what direction?

Star tried to quell the panic that was swelling in the group. She gestured emphatically at her headlamp. The message was clear. Search for the habitat, but stay in sight of the others' lights.

Okay, Adriana told herself, *you've got air left.* That was if she didn't squander it by breathing too fast. They retraced their steps a few hundred feet and fanned outward, scouring the bottom for the white ropes. The beam of Adriana's torch cast a ghostly oval over the reef, but she saw nothing but coral, sponges, and the occasional fish.

Come on! Where is it?

She took a quick inventory of her dive mates, now distant glows in the darkness. How would she even signal the others if she found something? Would a short, sharp shout into her regulator reach them?

It won't make any difference if we can't find something to shout about.

She could feel her gas running low now. There was still plenty to breathe, but it took more effort to suck it out of the tank. A check of the gauge drew a wheezing of shock from her. It was under 100 psi — at this depth, three minutes, tops! And she was gasping, devouring what little supply she had left.

Control yourself!

It was easier said than done. The full impact of their situation pressed down on her like the immense weight of the ocean. She couldn't shoot for the surface even if her tank ran bone dry. None of them could. The interns had been living at sixty-five feet for three days. Their bodies were saturated with dissolved nitrogen. A quick ascent would bring out millions of tiny gas bubbles, turning the blood into a lethal froth — a case of the bends so severe no one could survive it. Above lay only death.

But I'll suffocate!

Her face distorted by horror, she spun around to warn the others. Her panorama of black ocean revealed *two* sets of lights.

Two?!

Off to her left bobbed the interns' headlamps. And there, approaching fast from the right, were five more.

A rescue team?

But how did they know we were in trouble?

Right then, she didn't care. She pointed her DPV in the direction of the newcomers and took off.

As she closed the gap, she realized that she was advancing toward not a group of rescuers, but a single diver.

Dr. Delal! She came after all! And when she saw we weren't at the station, she went looking for us!

The newest aquanaut wore a headlamp and had strapped hand lights to both ankles and wrists to catch their attention in the dark sea. She looked bigger than Adriana remembered her — probably from the magnifying effect of the water.

Adriana drew a shallow, painful suck from her mouthpiece. Her gauge showed zero. She inhaled again —

Nothing! Terror twisted her insides. The tank was bone dry!

With two powerful kicks, the aquanaut was upon her. The newcomer wore smaller wing tanks affixed to arms and legs. Confident hands snapped one of the wings onto Adriana's regulator.

Air! The metallic tang of that first compressed lungful was the most delicious taste she could remember.

THE DEEP

"Thank you!" she panted into her mouthpiece.

Her savior was already steaming for the other three interns. Adriana followed. Even on her scooter, she had trouble keeping up with Dr. Delal's powerful kicks.

Kaz was beginning to panic, his gas supply dwindling. Dante, who was already out of air, was buddy-breathing what little Star had left. Adriana watched their rescuer distribute the wing tanks.

The truth was so awful it made her nauseous. But it was undeniable: If Igor Ocasek's replacement really had stayed topside until morning, they would all be dead.

It was a chastened and bone-weary team of interns that followed their rescuer back to PUSH. When the terror subsided, it left nothing but exhaustion in its wake. Adriana barely had the strength to haul her scooter, her burgeoning dive bag, and herself up the ladder to the wet porch.

She collapsed onto the plastic grating, fighting an impulse to weep with sheer relief. "Dr. Delal," she managed, too weak to pull off her gear, "I don't know what to say."

There was a familiar grunt that definitely couldn't have come from anyone named Jennifer. Up popped the mask to reveal the face of their savior.

It was English.

Menasce Gérard's dark, burning eyes scorched them with fury and contempt. "You!" the six-foot-five dive guide exclaimed. "They tell me only Jennifer is sick, I must go to PUSH in her place. If I know it is for you, I say no."

"Well, we're really glad you decided to come," Kaz said, his voice shaky. "We couldn't find the nav ropes. I don't know what happened."

"We messed up, pure and simple," Star confessed. "We could have died." She swallowed hard. "We *would* have died."

English was not sympathetic. "If you stop doing these idiot things, you do not have this problem! Night diving is not for the kindergarten. *Careful* — you have maybe heard this word before?"

"Sorry," mumbled Kaz.

"I am not Superman, me. I cannot always be there when you play dice with your lives. And for what?" He tossed a disgusted glance at Adriana's mesh bag, seeing the lumps of coral but not the artifacts they concealed. "Rocks. *Fou!*" He peeled off his dive gear and stormed through the pressure lock.

Dante set his tanks on the EMPTY rack by the compressor. "Is it just me, or is that guy always there every time we look like morons?"

THE DEEP

"Thank God for that," Kaz said feelingly. "How many times has he saved our necks?"

Adriana stepped out of her flippers. "Do you think he's right? Are the night dives too risky?"

Star shook her head vehemently. "We just got cocky, that's all. We made it okay a couple of times, and we let our guard down."

"Down here, you only get one mistake," Dante pointed out.

Star nodded gravely. "You're right. It was my bad, and it won't happen again. English is right. He won't be there for us every time."

"I don't want him *any* time," Dante said plaintively. "Don't get me wrong — I'm grateful. But he hates us."

"He doesn't hate us," argued Star.

"Ask him!" Dante insisted. "He doesn't even try to hide it."

"We'll stay out of his way," soothed Adriana.

"Down *here*?" Dante shrilled. "The guy takes up half the station! We couldn't stay out of his way if we shrank to the size of Barbie dolls! Face it — we're locked in an underwater sardine can with an unfriendly giant."

CHAPTER TEN

Menasce Gérard peered through the viewing port as the four interns set out from the station, gliding easily on their DPVs. He took careful note of the direction of their bubble trails, just in case he had to rescue them again.

He snorted. English was the most talented diver on an island of talented divers. His work on the oil rigs was difficult and dangerous, calling for great strength and skill at staggering depth and pressure. Why was a man like him playing nursemaid to a group of spoiled American teenagers?

He turned away from the viewing port. With a pop, his head shattered the bare bulb on the low ceiling. *Mon dieu*, this habitat was not built for a man his size! It was the interns who had brought him to this underwater dungeon, *merci beaucoup*.

As he brushed the glass fragments from his short hair, he noticed the crimson on his fingers. He began rummaging through the stainless steel cabinets in search of an adhesive bandage. An open cut was the last thing a diver needed. Even the slightest smell of blood in the water could attract sharks.

A lump of coral toppled from a cabinet and fell at his feet. Ah, yes — last night's souvenirs. Then he noticed the ancient piece of cutlery protruding from the small block. He examined the other contents of the locker, marveling at the artifacts inside. Those teenagers had found something! Was there no end to their mischief?

Within minutes, he was pulling on his wet suit. He selected a scooter from the rack, stepped down to the top rung of the ladder, and disappeared into the waiting water.

The interns cut power to their DPVs, gliding to a halt at the crater of shattered coral that was the wreck site.

Where was the boiling silt storm? More to the point, where were Reardon and the controlled devastation of the airlift?

Where was the *Ponce de León*?

Valving air into her B.C., Star ascended to forty feet — as high as she dared to go without risking decompression sickness. Sharp knives of sunlight cut the turquoise water, and she could clearly make out individual swells on the surface. Cutter's boat was nowhere to be seen.

After fumbling around in the pitch-black, skulking by headlamp, this felt almost like a promotion. Soon they were harvesting artifacts at greater speed than ever before, enjoying the excellent visibility and natural light.

Dante's sharp eyes made out a rounded edge. The photographer deftly plucked a pewter serving dish out of the debris and stuffed it in his bag. It was a nice find — the best of the day so far. But Dante wasn't satisfied.

Where's the money?

A Spanish galleon — the richest kind of shipwreck in the world. And what had the interns managed to salvage so far? Plates. Cups. Spoons. What were they supposed to do, have a tea party?

Of course he understood the archaeological value of these items. The stuff was a window back in time, three hundred years, maybe more.

Archaeology. That was Adriana's gig. Dante snorted into his mask — easy for her not to care about getting rich. She was rich already, or at least her family was. Dante might *need* that money someday. Photography probably didn't pay very well — black-and-white photography, anyway. And he was doomed to that specialty.

But with this treasure, or a share of it, he wouldn't have to care about that.

He finned away from the excavation, scanning the area. Maybe they were looking in the wrong place. Galleons were big, weren't they? What if they were working on the opposite end of the wreck from where the treasure had been stored? They could be salvaging some kind of seventeenth-century cafeteria while millions in silver, gold, and jewels lay a few yards off.

But where? And if the treasure lay buried under coral, how would they ever get at it? Cutter was the one with the airlift and the dynamite. Cutter had a boat that could winch anchors and cannon barrels up to the surface.

He stared at the reef's rocky rind, poring over every bump and contour. Surely, there had to be some sign, some hint of a man-made shape encased in the living limestone.

He found nothing.

He kicked through the murky haze stirred up by the efforts of the others, swimming to the far side of the wreck site. Here, coral gave way to sand and mud bottom.

Now that's searchable.

Expelling air from his vest, he dropped to the seafloor on his hands and knees and began to dig. Almost immediately, he was lost in his own silt cloud. As he labored, it occurred to him that if he'd thought to look here, so had Cutter.

Exhausted, and sucking far too much air, he

sat on the bottom in a remarkably dry-land pose, elbows on his knees, chin resting on his knuckles.

The picture came into focus gradually, as silt resettled itself, and the murky water began to clear around him. He blinked in surprise.

He'd always imagined the shoal as a broad plain, but really it was more of a mountainside here. Not far beyond the wreck site, the seafloor sloped sharply downward, falling off so quickly that Dante could not make out the bottom.

This is where the Hidden Shoals end. It must drop to deep ocean from here.

He increased buoyancy and lifted off the sand, peering into the abyss. As he floated free of the silt, the downward slope came into perfect focus. That was when he saw it.

It was far below on the incline, right at the point where the exhausted rays of sunlight succumbed to the permanent darkness of the deep. He could just make out the shadows of —

Of what?

He couldn't be sure. But it was definitely something. Half-buried objects, scattered along the distant slant as if they had bounced off the back of a runaway truck.

Could this be the treasure?

If I could only get a closer look . . .

Dante finned to the edge of the plateau, and

THE DEEP

angled his direction down, paralleling the slope of the bottom. Valving air out of his B.C. made descent easier, and he focused all his concentration on the faint hints of debris far below.

When he felt the tug on his leg, he yelped into his regulator, fearing the jaws of some prehistoric sea monster. No, it was another diver, waving a scolding finger.

Star?

He peered into the newcomer's mask and recoiled in shock. Oh, no! It was English, clinging to a DPV! The guide must have followed them. They were caught.

Dante held up a finger — one minute.

English shook his head vehemently. He pulled out his slate and scribbled: TOO DEEP.

PUSH aquanauts were supposed to maintain depth between forty and eighty feet. Dante checked his Fathometer. Almost ninety.

But I just need to see it!

Dante wheeled and continued to kick down the incline. English sprang into action. Dropping the scooter, he lunged forward, latching onto the boy's slim torso. Dante took evasive action, rolling out of his grasp. As English struggled to hold on, he accidentally yanked the boy's weight belt clean off.

Now suddenly buoyant, Dante shot upward. Desperately, he fumbled to deflate his B.C. to slow the ascent, but couldn't find the valve.

If I surface now, without decompression, the bends will kill me!

English's glove snapped out of nowhere and put an iron grip on his ankle. At last, Dante emptied his vest. Neutral again, he clamped himself onto the guide's arm and did not let go.

The weight belt floated to the sandy slope.

Clang.

The unmistakable sound reverberated under water, carrying even more clearly than it would have through the air.

Wait a minute. Lead weights hitting wet sand don't clang.

English heard it too. Both divers descended to the spot where the belt lay. The guide removed a flipper and shoveled through the mud and silt.

Dante spotted the dark object immediately. It was just below the sand, barely buried. The two wrested it free of the shoal, and English hefted it in his arms. It was about the size of a lampshade, dark with rust, and eaten through in about half a dozen places. But it was unmistakable — a brass bell.

The thoughts sparked instantly in Dante's

brain: Adriana! She had to see this! Old ships had bells, didn't they? Adriana would know if this was from a Spanish galleon.

A white-toothed grin penetrated English's perpetual scowl. He reached down and handed Dante his discarded weight belt. Dante reattached it, and the two kicked away in tandem, holding the bell between them like a trophy.

The dive guide's smile disappeared as they crested the slope. He took in the sight of the other three interns, busily harvesting artifacts from the ruined reef. They looked up at his approach, as though receiving his white-hot anger by telepathy.

Seething, English passed off the bell to Dante and swooped over the reef, examining the destruction. The strokes of the underwater pencil against his dive slate reverberated like gunshots.

YOU DO THIS?

Kaz blustered his denial, and wound up choking on salt water.

They were a hundred percent innocent, but how could they ever explain the whole story down here, where more than a syllable or two was impossible?

Star drew out her slate and wrote a single word: CUTTER.

English's stark expression plainly said he did not believe her.

At that moment, all explanation became unnecessary. Sixty-five feet overhead on the surface, a dark shape moved into position. Minutes later, an anchor dropped, settling on the reef ten yards away from them.

The *Ponce de León*.

The four interns retrieved their scooters and purred off to the ridge of coral that had served as their hiding place before. English followed, but his eyes never left the shadow of the research vessel above them.

They watched from the cover of the ridge as two dark figures descended through the filtered sunlight — divers wearing weighted boots instead of flippers. Chris Reardon and Tad Cutter. Instead of the long serpentlike tube of the airlift, each man carried what looked like a futuristic weapon, connected to the surface by a hose.

Kaz stared. What were those things? Dynamite charges? Spear guns? He did not have long to wait. The moment Reardon's boots thudded to the bottom, he positioned the six-inch blade against the unbroken reef at the edge of the excavation. With a monstrous roar, the device began pounding at the coral, smashing it to pieces.

Kaz gasped. A jackhammer! They were widening the search area!

Cutter's machine blasted to life, working on

the other side of the gash. Within seconds, the two treasure hunters disappeared inside an enormous cloud of silt and powdered coral.

Soon the interns couldn't see anything. But there was no question that the operation was proceeding. The vibration of the jackhammers seemed to rip at the very fabric of the ocean. At that, it was nothing compared to the vibrations of outrage emanating from Menasce Gérard. To a native islander, this wanton destruction of the living reef was nothing less than a crime against nature. It took every ounce of self-control he had, learned from a lifetime of diving, to hold himself back from physically attacking them.

Star understood his agitation. She scribbled on her slate and held it up for him to read:
TREASURE HUNTERS.

His expression thunderous behind his mask, English indicated Dante, who was close by, still hugging the bell. Their mesh bags bulged guiltily. The irony almost cut Kaz in two: *If Cutter's the treasure hunter, how come we have all the treasure?*

Mastering his anger at last, English turned his DPV back in the direction of PUSH and beckoned the others to follow.

They did not break free of the cloud kicked up

by the jackhammers until they were a third of the way home.

The wet porch rang with anxious voices.

"We didn't do anything to that coral!" Star pleaded their case. "Cutter broke it up with dynamite! We were just nosing around."

"This never was a real internship," Kaz continued. "The whole thing was a sham — a smokescreen to hide the fact that they were looking for a shipwreck."

"And they found it," Dante added. "Actually, *I* found it. But they stole it. And now they're digging up half the ocean looking for the treasure."

"It's the truth, Mr. English," Adriana said earnestly, "whether you believe us or not."

"I believe you," the guide said gravely.

They were struck dumb. It had never occurred to them that Menasce Gérard might take them at their word.

"Oh," said Kaz, surprised. "Great. So what happens now?"

The giant ignored him and pulled off his dive hood, checking the security of the Band-Aid on his head.

Dante spoke up. "You know — what's our next move? How do we stop Cutter?"

English shrugged hugely, his massive shoulders blotting out all view of the pressure hatch that led to the entry lock. "It is not my job for save the world, me."

"You mean you're just going to let him steal everything?" Dante protested.

English raised both expressive brows. "This is *my* property on the bottom of the ocean?"

"Well, shouldn't we at least call the cops?" asked Star. "That reef is protected, and they smashed it. They're smashing it *right now!*"

English laughed mirthlessly. "The cops — you refer to seven Saint-Luc men with the asthma. They cannot dive, so they are the cops."

"What about the government?" Adriana prompted.

"The government is eight thousand kilometers away, in Paris. The local magistrate is on Martinique, and would not know coral from corral, the place where you keep the horse." He looked earnestly into their faces. "*Tiens,* I agree with you. This is a terrible thing — a waste. But this is not my business. I am a diver. Justice is for someone else. A judge, *peut-être.*"

Dante hefted the bell. "Well, here's one thing Cutter's not going to get. What do you make of it, Adriana?"

She took it from him. It was heavier out of water, about the weight of a small TV. "It's the ship's bell, all right. We can try to clean off some of this rust. I think these things were engraved, so we might be able to identify the ship."

"For what?" grumbled Dante. "So Cutter can know whose gold he's getting rich on?"

"For historical value," Adriana insisted. "We know the artifacts are Spanish. Maybe the Spanish government keeps online archives we can check." She turned to English. "Do you think?"

"Why do you look at me?" the dive guide said, almost defensively. "What do I know about the Spanish treasure, me? A Frenchman named English."

The interns were taken aback. That was almost a *joke!* Humor from the implacable Menasce Gérard. It didn't seem possible.

"You know, you never explained that," Star ventured at last. "Where your name comes from, I mean."

"*Exactement*," English agreed. "I never explain you this thing."

He turned away to shrug out of his wet suit. And for a moment it seemed as if the subject was closed. But then the enormous guide spoke again.

"My ancestor was English," he said, his back still to them. "From the shipwreck."

THE DEEP

"Really?" Adriana was impressed. "How long ago?"

The famous shrug. "This is maybe, I think" — he paused, searching for the right word — "baloney? A rumor in the family. Here, *aux Antilles*, so many boats sink over the years, everybody think his ancestor sail with Columbus."

Kaz regarded English intently. "I know you don't like us because we don't belong at the institute. But now maybe you understand that it isn't our fault. We're not properly qualified because Cutter wanted us that way. He picked us because we're not great divers, and he picked Star because he thought she would be handicapped."

The guide tossed his wet suit onto the drying rack. He said, "You get better." And he ducked through the pressure hatch, leaving them alone.

The four interns stared from one to the other. First humor and now this. Had English actually said something *nice* to them?

CHAPTER ELEVEN

The old ship's bell, after more than three centuries at the bottom of the Caribbean, now sat in a glass tub, soaking in a mild acidic solution. On the other side of the lab area, in PUSH's entry lock, Adriana pounded the keyboard in search of clues to the identity of the mysterious galleon.

The lists and numbers that passed across the screen astonished her. The web site was maintained by the Spanish government. It contained a complete archive of every ship that had ever sailed to and from Spain, including its cargo. There were passenger manifests and bills of lading all the way back to the fifteenth century.

If that wreck is what we think it is, it has to be in here somewhere, Adriana reasoned.

Outside the viewing port by her shoulder, a lobster hunt was in progress. English was leading Star, Kaz, and Dante on a search for a dinner that was worthy of their last night on PUSH. Seafood was on the menu; peanut butter most definitely was not.

She got up from the chair and knelt down in front of the bell. Using a long-handled soft brush, she dabbed gently at the coating of rust on the brass. A cloud of reddish-brown particles flaked off into the surrounding liquid.

She squinted at the mottled surface. Was it getting cleaner, or was that just wishful thinking? She could make out faint lines of engraving, but nothing was clear enough to read.

She glanced up. Outside the porthole, Dante had cornered one of the clawless Caribbean lobsters in a rock crevice, and was trying to coax it out.

"Stay in there, kiddo," she advised the creature. "He wants to cook you." With a self-conscious laugh, she realized she had spoken aloud.

Dante lay on the rocks, his head almost completely inserted in the opening. As he reached out to grab, a huge dark shadow fell over him.

Adriana gaped. An enormous manta ray came flapping down to take a look at the diver with his head in a hole. Frantic, she banged on the window with both fists, hoping the concussion of her knocking would carry through the water. Perhaps it did, because Dante emerged with his captured lobster to find the twenty-foot wingspan of the devilfish looming over him.

Adriana couldn't hear anything, but it was

plain that Dante was screaming his head off. He spat out his regulator, and howled a cloud of bubbles that seemed to have no end. Star and Kaz tried to come to his aid, but Dante was out of control.

English finned onto the scene, with bubbles pouring from him as well. Adriana felt a stab of fear. The guide was afraid of nothing. Just how dangerous was this big beast that hovered like an alien spacecraft?

Then she realized that English was not in the grip of terror. He was laughing.

Somehow they managed to get Dante calmed down. He was inconsolable, though — in the excitement, his lobster had made its escape. With sign language, English instructed the others to watch. Then, astoundingly, he climbed right onto the manta's expansive back.

Adriana stared through the viewing port. The monster just hung there and allowed itself to be mounted, great wings undulating slightly. Then, with a nudge from its rider, it took off, sailing gracefully over the reef, bearing English like some begoggled jockey. It was out of Adriana's view almost immediately, but she could see the others watching with undisguised awe.

She returned her attention to the bell, and

brushed a little more. The solution was now growing cloudy with rust particles, and the engraving was definitely beginning to appear.

1! But no — there was a crosspiece on top! *T, then!* She dabbed the brush gently but firmly, holding herself back from scrubbing. If she ruined this artifact, she would never forgive herself.

T-O-L-L — no, the second L was an E!

Outside the habitat, the manta flashed by, this time with Star on its back. What was this — a carnival? Manta rides: fifty cents?

Concentrate! You're so close to cracking this!

She kept on working the soft bristles, and more engraving began to appear.

Another O. No, wait! It was a D! T-O-L-E-D — it could only be one word: Toledo!

Of course! All the great metalworks in Spain were in Toledo! This bell was made there!

The exhilaration of discovery had her dancing around the tiny room. But she quickly returned to the bell. There had to be a date there, and she was going to find it.

Star, Kaz, and Dante clattered onto the wet porch, whooping and exchanging high fives.

"That was awesome!" Star crowed ecstatically. "Like riding a pterodactyl underwater!"

"It was so *tame!*" marveled Dante. "Who

knew something that big and ugly could be so friendly?"

"Is that any way to talk about our dive guide?" Kaz grinned.

"You know what I mean!"

All at once, Adriana appeared at the pressure lock, smiling from ear to ear. She said, "*Nuestra Señora de la Luz.*"

The three stared at her.

"What are you babbling about?" asked Star.

"That's our galleon! It means 'Our Lady of the Light.' It sailed from Cádiz in 1648, and was lost at sea in 1665 on its fifth Atlantic crossing!"

"It says all that on the bell?" asked Dante incredulously.

Star was disgusted. "Sometimes you ask the dumbest questions! How could it say when they sank? You think they were engraving it while they were going down?"

"There are two inscriptions," Adriana explained breathlessly. "One says 'Toledo,' which means the bell was made at the metalworks there. And the other is '1648,' the year it was cast. I checked the old Spanish records. Seven new galleons were launched between 1648 and 1650. One of them burned in the harbor, and took the dock and half the town with it. One's on display at the Maritime Museum in Barcelona.

Two disappeared looking for the Philippines, which puts them ten thousand miles from here. Two were sunk in naval battles off the coast of Europe. That leaves just *Nuestra Señora de la Luz.*" She quivered with excitement. "It was part of the 1665 treasure fleet — the only ship that never made it home. According to the rest of the fleet, it disappeared in a hurricane in the French West Indies — right around here!"

"Then that's the only ship it can be!" Kaz exclaimed.

"And Cutter's taken it from us," added Star bitterly.

"Hold on a second," Dante interrupted. He turned to Adriana. "Did you say *treasure* fleet?"

"You won't believe it!" she crowed, eyes shining. "The web site showed the bills of lading. *Nuestra Señora* was a floating Fort Knox. You know that piece of eight we found? There were seven hundred thousand of them, freshly minted from South American silver! There were tons — *tons* — of gold! Chests piled high with pearls and precious stones! The total estimated value of that cargo today is one-point-two *billion* dollars!"

The whoop of celebration that escaped Dante was barely human.

"What are you so excited about?" asked Star.

"A billion bucks, and we've found nothing but a bunch of spoons and plates!"

"I think I know where the real thing might be!" Dante babbled excitedly. "If you go past the wreck site, the seafloor falls away to deeper ocean. The bell came from the top of that slope. But when I looked, I could see stuff scattered way, way down there, almost out of sight. The treasure's there! I know it!"

Adriana looked thoughtful. "It's possible, you know. *Nuestra Señora* went down in a hurricane. Heavy seas could have separated the cargo and dragged it off the shoal."

"We have to get to it before Cutter figures that out!" Kaz exclaimed urgently.

"I see," came a cold voice behind them.

They wheeled. English stood at the pressure hatch to the wet porch, scowling at them. Every inch of his six-foot-five frame radiated deep disapproval. He tossed a dive bag crawling with live lobsters onto the stainless steel counter.

"So. Monsieur Cutter, he is the treasure hunter. And you are not? You cry for the destruction of the reef, and then you drool over gold like common bank robbers! You do not fool me!"

Star was genuinely distressed. "That's not how it is!"

But English was carved from stone. "I have ears, me. I am not *stupide!*" With lightning speed, he reached out a hand and nudged an escaping lobster back into the bag. "Pack your gear. After dinner, we go into decompression. Then our association is at an end. Once we are topside, I do not know you."

The lobster was delicious, but the four interns very nearly choked on it. The click and scrape of cutlery on their plates resounded in the steel-trimmed galley. There was no conversation. Every time English cracked a shell, his expression plainly said he would have preferred to be snapping one of their necks.

It was painful, but not nearly as torturous as the endless stay in the decompression chamber. The only reading material was a small library of scientific journals. Every time one of the teens spoke, the dive guide would soon extinguish the conversation with a look that would have melted the polar ice cap. Kaz made an attempt to start a word game, but the other three were too intimidated to join in. Sleep was reduced to a handful of claustrophobic catnaps. The metal floor of the chamber was painful, but not half as much as the burning of the twin laser beams of English's eyes.

Over seventeen agonizing hours, the device

brought them back to surface pressure, giving their bodies a chance to expel the excess nitrogen they had absorbed during their time at sixty-five feet.

At long last, they wordlessly gathered together their tiny pieces of luggage, their bags of artifacts, and the *Nuestra Señora* bell, and started up the habitat's umbilical to the PUSH life-support buoy. Sunlight had never seemed so overpoweringly brilliant. There, waiting for them, was the *Hernando Cortés*. Captain Vanover was on the dive platform to haul them aboard.

"Hey, you guys, how was it? Iggy said you were having a blast!"

Star kicked off her flippers. "Yeah, well, Iggy left," she said pointedly.

Vanover frowned. "Huh?"

English surfaced behind them, deliberately swam away from the platform, reached up to the forward gunwale, and hoisted himself aboard. He peeled back his hood, stepped out of his fins, and stormed below, without a word to anyone.

CHAPTER TWELVE

To tell or not to tell. That was the question.

One thing was certain: The interns had come up against a brick wall. Now that their stay at PUSH was over, they no longer had access to the wreck site. And they definitely had no way to investigate what Dante had spotted on the deep-water slope at the edge of the Hidden Shoals.

The next morning, in search of privacy, the four signed out bicycles and took to the dirt path that connected Saint-Luc's tiny villages.

"We need help," Kaz concluded, propping his bike up against a rock. "And that means we have to spill the beans to somebody. Who do we trust?"

Star laughed mirthlessly. "My mother, but she's not here."

Adriana adjusted her kickstand. "It has to be the captain," she reasoned. "English hates us, Gallagher ignores us, Cutter's the enemy, and Marina's with Cutter."

"We can't trust anybody," Dante said flatly. "Not with a billion dollars."

DIVE

"Then it stays down there," Kaz argued. "And what good is that?"

Dante squinted out over the vast expanse of ocean visible from high ground. "How well do we really know the captain? So he's a nice guy — so what? He could be in cahoots with Cutter. Or he could use our info to buy his way on to Cutter's team."

"Maybe," Star nodded. "But I don't think so."

"Let's put it to a vote," decided Kaz. "Who says the captain's in?" He raised his hand. Adriana was next, followed by Star.

Dante was distraught. "Do you guys realize how many zeroes there are in a billion?"

"If you're so good at math," Star pointed out, "then you know you've already lost this election."

Painfully, Dante's hand crept up to join the others. "I hope we're not sorry about this."

"You're absolutely positive you've found *Nuestra Señora de la Luz?*" asked Captain Vanover.

They sat on aluminum folding chairs, sinking into the sandbar where the portable restaurant was located. *La Mouette,* translation "The Seagull," was established every morning at low tide in six inches of water on the soft shoal about a hundred feet off the beach at Côte Saint-Luc. It could only be reached by rowboat or motorized launch. And it had to be dismantled every afternoon before high tide. But the spot could not be more spectacular, with gentle whitecaps breaking all around, and thousands of gulls and pelicans lighting on the glistening water.

The captain had invited the four interns to be his guests at lunch. They were ignored by Dr. Gallagher, avoided by Cutter and his crew, and despised by Menasce Gérard. Someone, he felt, had to be nice to them. "People have been looking for that ship for three hundred years."

"We're positive," Adriana confirmed. "Every single artifact we took from the wreck was Spanish — all except for the JB hilt, which someone must have stolen or traded for, I guess. And according to the Spanish records, there's only one galleon it could be."

"If you're right, you're rich," said Vanover.

"Or Cutter is," added Dante mournfully.

Vanover scowled. It had been hard for him to believe that Tad Cutter, a Poseidon scientist, was abusing his credentials in order to hunt for treasure. But earlier that day, Menasce Gérard had said the same thing. "I should have listened to you the first time you told me he was up to no good. But I don't think he's found any more than you have yet. I'd notice if the *Ponce de León* had a heavy load in its hold. She'd wallow to the gun-wales."

"Then there's still time," urged Kaz. "Come with us when we tell Gallagher! He won't listen to us, but he'll have to pay attention to one of his own captains."

Vanover took a bite of his seafood stew and chewed thoughtfully. "We could try that. But what good would it do? Poseidon fires Cutter — and then what? He'll just find another boat and keep digging. Right now you have a real advantage over him. He doesn't know that you know."

"And he doesn't consider us a threat," added Adriana.

"He doesn't consider us at all," Star said bitterly.

"That's a plus," Vanover pointed out. "Right now he must be banging his head against the wall, wondering where the treasure is. In his wildest dreams, he'd never believe you kids are as close to it as he is."

"Maybe even closer," Kaz told him. Slowly, he explained Dante's sighting of what looked like a trail of scattered objects, and his idea that the treasure might lie down there. "It's just a theory," Kaz finished, "but Dante's never been wrong about what he sees underwater."

THE DEEP

The captain sat forward. "How deep was it?"

"I was at ninety feet when I spotted it," Dante replied. "And it's hard to judge, but it looked a whole lot farther away than the surface. English was with me, and he didn't see anything."

Vanover whistled between his teeth. "Sounds like two-fifty, three hundred feet. Out of diving range — at least, with standard scuba. But we might still be able to take a look."

"How?" asked Star.

"Don't ask me." Vanover sat back and grinned. "Ask an old friend of yours."

Dr. Igor Ocasek was thrilled to see them, and even happier to be asked for his expertise. "I'm kind of at loose ends while my lab is being repaired," he explained.

The problem: how to examine a seafloor too deep for conventional diving.

The solution: lower a video camera to three hundred feet, and look around from the safety and comfort of the R/V *Hernando Cortés*.

The eccentric scientist was already making notes before they had finished telling him what they wanted.

"You'll require floodlights at that depth," he decided, "so there should be some kind of mounting platform. And weights for stability. Let's see

— four wide-angle cameras will provide a three-hundred-and-sixty-degree sweep. Three hundred feet of coaxial cable — no, better make it four hundred. Wouldn't want to be caught short if we have to go deeper —"

"Don't you want to know what we need it for?" asked Kaz in amazement.

"Mmmmm."

And then there were six people on the face of the earth who knew about the mysterious objects on the edge of the Hidden Shoals.

The more the information spread, the greater the chance that someone would betray the secret. But the interns had no choice. Dr. Ocasek had to be aware of what he was looking for.

When they told him, he hardly even looked up. One-point-two billion dollars was the same as one-point-two cents to a man who cared only for science.

30 August 1665

If Samuel had thought the surrender meant the end of the bloodshed, he was sorely mistaken. Now in firm control of the settlement, the privateers went completely berserk. For nearly four months they had been trapped aboard ship — mistreated, malnourished, and, on top of their discomfort, bored to the brink of insanity. Now this sealed cauldron of frustrated energy boiled over onto the hapless citizens of Portobelo.

The cruelty was beyond imagination. As the towering sails of the privateer fleet moved into the captured harbor, screams rang out from every house in the shattered town. Even the church was no sanctuary. Torture and murder became an entertainment. Looting followed naturally, as the dead had no use for possessions. Every ring, every bracelet, every cross, even of base metal, found its way into an English pocket.

Samuel was assigned to York to help with the wounded privateers. The barber was in his customary condition — blood-soaked. The saw he used for his terrible amputations looked like a utensil from a slaughterhouse.

Samuel hated any time he was forced to spend with York. But today it was a mercy, because it kept him away from the plunder and carnage all around him.

Right now York was attending to Patchett. The chief gunner had sustained a sword slash to the shoulder. It was almost a stroke of good luck. A few inches lower, and the man would certainly have lost his arm to York's saw. But a shoulder could not be amputated. It had to be treated, and the treatment was this:

The barber brought out a small tin from the pocket of his greasy vest and handed it to Samuel. As Patchett howled in agony, York reached filthy fingers into the wound and separated the torn flesh. It was Samuel's job to pour the contents of the tin into the long cut.

Samuel lifted the tin and recoiled in revulsion. Instead of healing powder, the container was crawling with maggots.

"Sir!" he cried. "The worms have eaten the medicine!"

York roared with laughter. "The worms are the medicine, Lucky! They'll eat the bad flesh and leave the good intact. Now pluck out four lively ones and drop them inside."

THE DEEP

Samuel did as he was told, then ran behind the back of the Casa Real and vomited until there was nothing left to come up.

Then the shouting began, Captain Blade's voice louder than any other. Samuel followed the sound, fully aware that he should probably be running in the opposite direction. The throng of privateers was assembled in front of the large storehouses at the waterfront. The wealth of the New World was collected in these buildings — precious metals from the mines of the natives to the south, and unimaginable riches from the Orient. The treasure was carried overland by mule train from Panama on the Pacific side of the isthmus to this very spot. Here it waited for the great galleons to convey it to the Spanish king.

Samuel had heard the sailors of the Griffin speak of this place on their journey. It was, quite simply, the richest acre on the face of the earth.

The huge doors had been thrown open, revealing the contents of the legendary storehouses. Even from a distance, Samuel could see that they were all empty.

He had witnessed many displays of ill temper and homicidal rage during his time as James Blade's cabin boy. But never had he seen his captain in such a state. The mayor of Portobelo cowered on the ground before him, offering information in exchange for his life.

"The galleons, they leave — four days since! Take all treasure! We hide nothing! I swear!"

Captain Blade drew out his lash, and the mayor shrank away in terror. The whip cracked — not at the pitiful Spaniard, but over the heads of the privateer crew. It was a call to attention.

"Back to the ships, you scurvy rats! Those galleons are wallowing low with our treasure! Keep your swords handy, lads! The killing's not over yet!"

THE DEEP

CHAPTER THIRTEEN

By the light of the moon, the *Hernando Cortés* chugged quietly out of Côte Saint-Luc harbor, just before eleven o'clock. There were no witnesses. But even if the departure had been observed, it was unlikely that anyone would have been able to identify the apparatus lashed to the foredeck.

The thing looked like the window display of a camera store that had been struck by lightning, fusing cameras and floodlights into a tightly packed mass.

"Does it work?" asked Adriana timidly.

Dr. Ocasek seemed vaguely surprised at the question. "It worked perfectly in my bathtub."

At the wheel, Vanover brayed a laugh. "Don't worry. If Iggy built it, it'll fly." He frowned as the vessel bounced through the oncoming waves. "Choppy tonight. We could be in for a rough ride."

When they reached the coordinates of the wreck site, Vanover cut their speed. They proceeded slowly until the sonar told them that they were passing over the point where the Hid-

DIVE

den Shoals sloped down to deeper ocean. Dr. Ocasek's camera array was then winched up and over the side. As it disappeared beneath the surface, the floodlights came on. Everyone gasped. The illumination was so powerful that the sea lit up like an aquarium. The light dimmed as the contraption descended. But even at the search depth of 250 feet, the watchers could still make out a faint glow coming from beneath the waves.

The four interns rushed below to the closed-circuit monitor Dr. Ocasek had set up in the salon. The screen was split in four, one quadrant for each camera.

Dante frowned. "There's nothing."

The screen showed swirling water and an occasional sea creature staring in surprise at this bizarre mechanical intruder.

"We're off the reef," Dr. Ocasek reminded him. "That's where the densely packed marine life is."

"But where's the bottom?" asked Star.

"I'm not sure," said Dr. Ocasek.

"Picture a mountain," came Captain Vanover's voice through the two-way radio from the wheelhouse. "Our cameras are sort of floating in space beside it. This slope might not bottom out flat for two or three thousand feet."

Kaz felt his eyelids beginning to droop. Fifteen minutes of staring at nothing was taking its toll on all the interns as the clock ticked on past midnight. This was turning into a big bust. How could anyone find something on the slope if they couldn't even find the slope itself?

It came up so fast that they barely had a chance to scream. First a large luminescent jellyfish flashed through the top right quadrant. Then a diagonal wall of sand and seaweed was hurtling toward the camera.

Dante reacted first. "Hit the brakes!" he bellowed at the walkie-talkie.

"Slow down!" cried Adriana.

"Veer off!" shouted Star.

When the camera struck the mud, Kaz flinched, expecting an impact. But of course the boat hadn't struck anything. Only the camera array, 250 feet below the surface, had suffered a collision.

Following Dr. Ocasek's instructions, Vanover reversed course, and the contraption came free of the muddy incline. Two lenses were sand-encrusted, but soon washed clean.

From that point on, no one felt remotely sleepy or bored. The *Cortés* traced slow track lines across the water, allowing the cameras a chance to scan the gradient for five hundred yards in each horizontal direction. Then the winch would lower the array another twenty-five feet, Captain Vanover would adjust course, and the thousand-foot trace would begin again.

Around 2 A.M., while they were lowering the array to 325 feet, a gusty wind blew up in their faces, and rain began to pelt down on them.

"How much longer is this going to take?" yelled Vanover from the cockpit. "We've got weather coming!"

With the rough wave action tossing its umbilical line, the camera array bounced and spun far below them. The pictures were chaotic. Kaz's head pounded as he stared at the screen, fearful that something might go by undetected. The motion of the boat was making him queasy, and he swallowed determinedly, his eyes glued to the monitor. Beside him, Dante, never a good sailor, was hugging his knees and moaning.

Dr. Ocasek was the picture of total focus. "If it's down there, we'll find it," he said calmly.

When the time came to lower the winch to 350 feet, it was obvious that conditions outside had deteriorated even further. The tossing of the deck knocked Adriana flat on her back. Even Kaz, who had superb balance from hockey, had to hold on to cabin tops and bulwarks as the sea manhandled the *Cortés*.

"Get back below!" shouted Vanover from be-hind the wheel. "I'm turning us around!"

"Not yet!" begged Dante, screaming to be heard over the wind. "I *know* I saw something!"

"No!" boomed the captain. "In these seas, if you go overboard, you're done!"

A wave broke over the bow, drenching the winch and the interns who struggled to man it.

"Just one more track line!" howled Star, shak-ing herself like a wet dog. "If we give up now, we'll never finish this!"

Vanover hesitated, the driving rain stinging his face. "One more!" he agreed finally. "But then I don't care if you find the lost continent of Atlantis — we're going home!"

Star and Dante sloshed down the companion-way, and joined the others in front of the monitor for the last pass.

The ship lurched, and a moment later, the camera array swung away from the slope below. And when the pendulum effect brought the appa-ratus back into position, there it was in the bottom left quadrant:

The long bronze barrel of a cannon.

All four interns began screaming at the same time. Not one word was intelligible.

Even Dr. Ocasek was excited. "Back up, Braden! Back up!"

"Are you crazy?" crackled the sharp voice through the two-way radio. "It's all I can do to keep us afloat!"

The array bobbed in the current, and for an instant, one of the cameras dipped down to reveal a scattering of ballast stones and other debris half buried on the sandy slope.

Dante was out of his seat, crying, *"Did you see that?"* until a sudden pitch of the boat sent him sprawling into Dr. Ocasek's arms.

"It's more debris from *Nuestra Señora!*" exclaimed Adriana in amazement. "I wonder how it got all the way over here."

Star had an idea. "Maybe the galleon broke in two when it sank. And the force of the hurricane blew half of it off the shoal."

"The half with the money in it!" Dante added breathlessly.

Kaz warmed to the argument. "It would explain why Cutter hasn't found any treasure."

"Hey!" came an angry shout from the radio. Then, "If you guys are finished theorizing, do I have your permission to get us out of here?"

"Go!" urged Dr. Ocasek. "We'll bring up the camera array so it doesn't get smashed to pieces when we cross the reef."

"Okay, but *be careful!* We're taking ten-foot waves over the bow."

THE DEEP

By the time they got topside, the deck of the *Cortés* was awash with foam and reeling from the motion of the sea. A stack of safety harnesses came sailing down from the wheelhouse and splashed at their feet.

"Get in them!" boomed Vanover. "And lash yourselves to something permanent!"

The thirty-foot walk to the winch was as tough an obstacle course as Kaz could remember. He clipped himself to the rail and hung on for dear life as Dr. Ocasek started the winch. The cable began to wind up.

Kaz put out a hand as Star stumbled. A second later, his own legs slipped out from under him, and he dangled from his harness, knowing he would have been swept away without it. Star, on the other hand, had kept her feet and was sneering triumphantly down at him.

The winch continued to shudder and groan. Two hundred feet . . . a hundred and fifty . . . The underwater lights grew nearer and brighter as they rose. The violent ocean began to glow beneath them. One hundred feet . . . fifty . . . twenty-five . . .

And then the array, still lashed to its weighted platform, broke the surface. Brilliant as a supernova, it turned night into day, showing the occupants of the *Hernando Cortés* just how much trouble they were in. The heeling of the boat in the troughs and crests of the oncoming seas had turned the dangling array into a hundred-pound projectile. It swung from the tip of the winch's crane arm like a lethal tetherball, smacking into the side of the wheelhouse and shattering a porthole. Then the craft righted itself, sending the contraption across the full beam of the ship, missing Adriana's head by inches.

Kaz grabbed a boathook and snagged the umbilical. But the next movement of the ship ripped the pole out of his hands.

"Heads up!" boomed Vanover as the array sailed back over them.

Wham! It connected with the railing, denting it. They watched as one of the cameras, jarred loose by the impact, pitched into the sea.

Kaz picked up the boat hook and swung it at the twisting umbilical. He missed the cable, but the end caught the neck of one of the floodlights and clamped on. The whole array came crashing to the deck.

With a cry like a springing tiger, Dr. Igor Ocasek flung himself on top of his runaway creation, preventing it from sailing off again.

It was 4:30 A.M. by the time the *Hernando Cortés* limped back to Côte Saint-Luc harbor.

THE DEEP

Waterlogged and weary, the four interns helped Dr. Ocasek carry what was left of the array back to the scientist's cabin. One camera was missing, one was smashed, several floodlights were shattered, and the whole arrangement was covered in mud from numerous collisions with the sloped seabed.

"Sorry about this, Iggy," Star said sheepishly. "I didn't think we were going to wreck it."

Dr. Ocasek was upbeat. "We found what we were looking for. That's all that matters. The rest was the weather's fault."

"You're not going to get into any trouble for this, are you?" asked Dante nervously.

"Are you kidding?" The scientist grinned. "If I showed up one day and everything *wasn't* broken, Geoffrey would have a heart attack!"

They said good night and trudged off to their own quarters. Kaz and Dante let themselves into their cabin and switched on the light.

Dante went straight to the bathroom and began peeling off his wet clothes. "I've never been so tired in my life! I'm going to sleep for a hundred years!"

"Join the club," yawned Kaz. "The minute I hit that pillow — " He froze.

There in the corner sat the bell of *Nuestra Señora de la Luz*, cushioned by a bath mat. It was partly off the piece of cloth, which meant it had been moved. And, on the terrazzo floor in front of it, facing it, were two sandy footprints.

Maybe their activities weren't such a secret from Cutter after all.

CHAPTER FOURTEEN

It was almost noon before Adriana awoke, the powerful Caribbean sun threading through the gap in the curtains and all but searing a hole in the center of her forehead. She looked to the other bed. Star was still asleep, snoring softly into her pillow. Divers always snored. It was a side effect of time spent at depth and pressure. Even Adriana had woken herself a few times with a loud snort.

She sat up, yawning and stretching, then caught a glimpse of her hands, and gasped aloud. Thick brown mud was caked under all ten fingernails. Her immaculate, stylish mother would faint dead away!

Ballantyne ladies see to their grooming. Adriana had been hearing that since birth. Mother, obviously, had never had to handle a hundred-pound camera array that had scoured the seafloor. To her, the purpose of the ocean was for cruising, and to supply sushi.

She padded barefoot into the small bathroom, and switched on the light. Digging through her

DIVE

toiletry bag, she came up with her manicure set and began to clean her nails.

Yuck! This job is disgusting. You could plant potatoes in the blob I just excavated from under my thumbnail!

And then the blob twinkled.

Huh? Adriana blinked.

It was a tiny particle in the dirt, about half the size of a grain of sand. It was bright yellow, and when it caught the light, it gleamed.

She looked closer. Not yellow, exactly. More like — gold.

Intrigued now, she spread a tissue on the counter, popped the dirt onto it, and used an eyebrow tweezers to separate the shiny fleck from the rest of the material.

It was very shiny — and soft, too. The sharp tweezers could not cut the particle. Strong pressure just left an indentation.

Her breath caught. This didn't just look like gold; it *was* gold!

She finished cleaning her nails onto the tissue, and examined the results. Only dirt. Head spinning, she sat down on the edge of the tub, trying to sort out her thoughts. The dirt under her nails came from carrying Iggy's camera array. That was mud dredged up from the sloping ocean floor near the second debris field from *Nuestra Señora*. How could it be a coincidence — a tiny piece of gold from the very spot where they suspected a vast treasure lay hidden?

But Spanish gold came in bars, coins, great decorative chains. This was barely larger than a particle of dust.

When the answer came to her, it brought with it so much adrenaline that the feeling was closer to terror than understanding. She leaped to her feet, unable to contain the excitement within one body.

"Star! — *Star!!*"

At a quiet corner table in the Poseidon cafeteria, the four interns met with Captain Vanover.

Dante stared at the tiny fleck on Adriana's fingertip. "That's not treasure! That's a molecule!"

"It's a *gold* molecule," Star said in irritation. "And keep your voice down."

"It *is* pretty small," Vanover pointed out. "I can't explain it, but I guess there's a chance it occurs naturally."

"I thought so too," said Adriana. "But then I remembered something I read on the Spanish government web site. All treasure arriving in Spain from the New World was heavily taxed.

But you could never know how much more was smuggled in to avoid the taxes. And the easiest treasure to sneak past the authorities was gold dust."

"Yeah," said Kaz dubiously, "but one piece?"

Star took up the explanation. "Think about what happens when a boat sinks. It creates a whirlpool effect, like the *Titanic*. Something as light as gold dust would get sucked up into the whirlpool, and end up spread out all over the bottom around the wreck."

"So we tried a little experiment," Adriana took up the tale. "We pulled all our muddy clothes out of the hamper. And there was another speck on Star's shirt." Her eyes shone. "We're not wrong about this. The debris field we photographed last night has the treasure in it — the *real* treasure! We can't get at all that dust, but the rest of it is lying there, just waiting to be claimed!"

Dante choked back a whoop. "I can't believe it! We found it! It's ours! Now all we have to do is figure out how to bring it up."

"Not so fast," the captain said seriously. "What we saw last night was at three hundred and fifty feet. And that was just the top of the debris field. Who knows how much farther down

THE DEEP

the slope the treasure could be? There's no way I can let you kids — even you, Star — dive so deep."

Star's jaw stiffened. "That's not your decision to make! No offense, Captain — you've been great to us. But we're talking about a billion dollars here!"

"It isn't worth a dime if you get yourself killed going after it."

Dante was horrified. "You mean we're just going to *leave* it there?"

"Calm down," Vanover soothed. "There are ways to salvage things from deep water. It's possible, but it's tricky. And you have to know exactly what you're doing. Take it easy. We've got time. Cutter's looking in the wrong place; and he doesn't know that you guys are looking at all."

Kaz and Dante exchanged a worried look. "That's not exactly true," Kaz began slowly. He told the others about finding the footprints on the cabin floor in front of the bell. "We have to assume it's Cutter," he finished. "Who else could it be?"

Star looked alarmed. "That's trouble. If he sees us nosing around the second debris field, we'll be leading him right to the treasure."

Captain Vanover looked like a man who had just made up his mind. "All right — here's what we're going to do. Poseidon maintains a research sub called *Deep Scout*. I'm going to requisition it, and we're all going down there. If we can snag a piece of that treasure and match it to the cargo list on the web site, we can file a claim on the wreck with the International Maritime Commission." He made eye contact with all four. "Then it won't matter what Cutter knows. It'll be our prize, not his."

CHAPTER FIFTEEN

If a bubble helicopter married a submarine, their offspring might look very much like the DSV *Deep Scout*. A gleaming sphere made of clear acrylic sprouted from a titanium hull that was pockmarked with lights, cameras, and other instruments. Six folded manipulator arms gave the submersible an almost insectlike appearance.

"Isn't she beautiful?" crowed Captain Vanover.

"No," said Dante with conviction.

"I guess not," the captain conceded. "But she'll take us where we need to go. Besides, this boat is usually booked six months in advance. You kids have no idea how many favors I had to call in and people I had to lie to in order to get us on the schedule on such short notice."

Deep Scout sat on the launch deck of its support vessel. *Scoutmaster* was a much larger ship than the *Hernando Cortés* or the *Ponce de León*. It had to be to house the crane mechanism required to place the deep-sea vehicle in the water, and to pluck it out again when the mission was done.

DIVE

Kaz's head was spinning by the end of the handshakes and introductions. "It takes this many guys to run one little submersible?" he whispered.

"Most of these are *Scoutmaster's* crew," Vanover replied. "But there's always a tech on board monitoring the sub's every move. Remember, *Deep Scout* was built to explore the ocean floor at depths of up to two miles." Seeing Dante turn gray, he added quickly, "We won't be going *that* far down."

Vanover left them and climbed the metal ladder to the big ship's towering bridge. It was his job to direct *Scoutmaster's* captain to the correct coordinates where Dr. Ocasek's camera array had spotted the second debris field.

Dante leaned against the rail, observing the beehive of activity. "You think we're going to have to split the money with all these people?"

Adriana was disgusted. "Is that all this is to you? Money?"

"Yeah, well, maybe those of us who don't already have one-point-two billion dollars are kind of looking forward to seeing how the other half lives," Dante shot back.

Her eyes narrowed in anger. "You have no way of knowing how much my family has or doesn't have."

"You don't have to apologize for being rich,"

Dante insisted. "But don't act all superior because you're in this for pure archaeology. It's easy to be high-minded when you don't need the money. I do."

"I don't care about the money," Star put in grimly. "I just want to see the look on Cutter's face when we show up with that treasure. Us — the losers he picked because we wouldn't be a threat . . . the *cripple* who couldn't possibly dive. . . ." Her voice trailed off, but her eyes were blazing. "I just want to see that."

Money. Science. Revenge. Kaz marveled at the different reasons his fellow interns had for coveting this treasure. His mind was on something else entirely — the skull they had unearthed at Cutter's excavation. More than three hundred years ago, people had perished in this shipwreck.

And we're going to take their stuff because they're in no shape to protect it anymore.

The logic was ridiculous. All the gold in the world wouldn't help those poor sailors, three centuries dead, their descendants scattered across dozens of generations.

Besides, if we don't get that treasure, Cutter will.

His reverie was interrupted by Vanover's call from the bridge. "Show time, folks!"

If *Scoutmaster's* deck was busy and frenetic, the cabin of the submersible was an incredibly lonely place. When the hatch was sealed, the five-inch-thick acrylic bubble blotted out all sound. It was like being shut inside a glass tomb. They were immersed in *Deep Scout's* titanium hull up to chest level. Above that, the sphere created a greenhouse effect. Brilliant sunlight baked the cramped interior.

"It cools off when you dive," the captain promised. He was flipping toggle switches and adjusting dials on a control panel that wrapped around the pilot's chair.

That was the only official seat. The four interns pressed into the rest of the cabin, an area of deck space about four feet wide and six feet long. It reminded Kaz of the famous college prank to see how many students would fit into a Volks-wagen.

At last, all was in readiness. "Topside, this is *Scout*," Vanover said into the microphone. "Ready to rock."

It was an eerie feeling — motion, but no sound — as the huge A-frame crane hoisted the vehicle over the side and placed it almost gently in the water. The interns felt rather than heard the waves smacking against the hull. There was a grating sensation as the drop-lock disengaged.

And then *Deep Scout* sank into the deep of the Caribbean.

Clear water changed from pale turquoise to blue, and finally to blue-black. Vanover activated the outside floodlights, and the dark sea around them came alive. Curious fish circled this strange titanium wanderer, drawn by the rhythmic pings and pops of the submersible's acoustic tracking system. Others, bioluminescent jellyfish and octopuses, gave the newcomer a wide berth.

"Awesome," breathed Star, bathed in the reddish glow of the control panels.

"You never get used to it," the captain told her, his eyes darting back and forth from the undersea panorama to the data screen over his shoulder.

Deep Scout was designed to operate miles below the surface, so it reached the slope at the edge of the Hidden Shoals very quickly. Captain Vanover manipulated the thrusters, and they began to track back and forth across the incline, searching for the debris field they had only glimpsed through Dr. Ocasek's cameras.

An hour later, they had still found nothing.

Star was growing edgy. "I don't get it. We have to be in the right place. GPS coordinates don't lie."

"We're going by the coordinates of the

Cortés," the captain reminded her. "Remember, the camera array was at the end of a four-hundred-foot tether, blowing around in a storm. We can't know exactly where it was when it detected the debris." He was trying to sound confident, but the strain was evident in his voice. He had gone out on a limb to book *Deep Scout*. If they came up empty-handed, it could cost him his career.

All at once, Dante lurched forward, bonking his head on the thick acrylic of the sphere. "There!"

"Where?" cried the other four in unison.

"Down there!"

Vanover dumped air from the ballast tanks, and the submersible descended. The Fathometer gave their depth as 344 feet. And suddenly, there it was in the lights — the long bronze cannon.

"Look!" Adriana pointed. "The ballast stones!"

They were scattered along the slanting seafloor below the corroded barrel, disappearing into the inky depths.

"Wow," Kaz said, nearly overwhelmed. "How far do they go?"

"Only one way to find out." The captain operated the thrusters. *Deep Scout*'s nose dipped, and the submersible followed the slope down.

The ballast stones were still there at four hundred feet. And at five hundred. In fact, the spread of debris seemed to be thickening. As they passed through six hundred, they could make out other signs of the shipwreck — plates, bottles, muskets, helmets. Intermingled with these items was something the interns had not seen before.

"Are those *timbers*?" Dante asked incredulously, his face pressed up against the acrylic of the sphere.

Vanover nodded. "Wood can't survive up on the reef, where the worms eat it. But the deeper you go, the sea life is less dense, and the old ships last longer — especially the parts that are buried in sand."

"That's an awful lot of stuff for one ship," observed Star. "Remember, half of it's up on the reef. This debris has to stop somewhere."

Dante saw it first, but a moment later, *Deep Scout's* lights illuminated it for the others. About thirty feet below them, the slope suddenly flattened out before dropping off again. This tilted plateau, seven hundred feet beneath the waves, was the final resting place of the old ship.

Kaz stared. It was uncanny how sure of it he felt. Naturally, there was no abandoned galleon listing there on the shelf. Yet the mound of debris half buried in the ancient sand was shaped exactly like an old boat, bloated by slow collapse over the centuries. As the vehicle drew closer, they could make out anchors and cannons — even some of the wooden spine of a once-proud sailing vessel.

There was only one thing that didn't make sense. "That's a whole ship," Kaz mused with a frown. "Or most of it, anyway. How did a piece end up all the way over on the reef where Cutter's digging?"

"There's no way this is the same boat," the captain decided. "Crazy as it seems, you kids found *two* shipwrecks, not just one."

Adriana's eyes shone with excitement. "*Two* shipwrecks!"

"No!" Dante was alarmed. "*Nuestra Señora* was the ship with the money! *That's* what we need, not some old garbage scow that happened to sink next door!"

"Besides," put in Star, "what about the gold dust test? That said the treasure was *here*, not up on the reef."

The acoustic tracker *pinged* as the five thought it over.

Captain Vanover spoke at last. "Let's give these manipulators a workout. If we come up with a gold ingot, it won't make any difference what ship we're pulling it out of." Skillfully, he dumped air and worked the thrusters until *Deep Scout* hovered directly over the remains of the old ship. Then he reached for the controls that operated the submersible's mechanical arms.

The shape that exploded out of the darkness was longer than the submersible itself, a living missile of pure speed and energy. Kaz saw the eye first, blank and staring, a shiny black button the size of a clenched fist. He recognized the creature instantly, even before the enormous mouth gaped open, revealing row upon lethal row of crushing, ripping teeth.

Although he was safe behind five inches of solid acrylic, Kaz felt the terror course through his body. For such an array of weaponry could only belong to one fish in these waters.

It was Clarence, the monster tiger shark that had nearly taken his life three weeks earlier.

And before Kaz had time to scream, the two-ton body hurtled into the side of *Deep Scout*.

CHAPTER SIXTEEN

The vehicle lurched from the collision, tossing its occupants like socks in a dryer.

"It's —" Before Kaz could make the identification, he smacked heads with Adriana and went down hard.

"Clarence!" Dante rasped, picking himself up off the deck. "He's trying to eat the sub!"

"Hang on, people!" ordered Vanover, clinging to the controls. "He can't hurt us in here!"

At that moment, the enormous shark struck the hull again, knocking *Deep Scout* over on its side. Kaz was pressed against the glass, his face contorted with fear.

"Yeah, well, he's doing a pretty good job of it!" Dante cried, steadying himself on the pilot's seat.

The captain fired thrusters in an attempt to stabilize the vehicle. "He can kick us around a bit. He's as big as the boat. But a shark can't bite through titanium. Or bulletproof plastic," he added as the blunt snout the size of a cocktail table pummeled the acrylic sphere.

"I — " Kaz struggled to think rationally despite his terror. "I don't think he's trying to eat us. It's more like he's *fighting* us, pushing us away."

"Protecting his territory, almost," Adriana added.

"That's impossible," challenged Star. "Sharks don't live at seven hundred feet, do they?"

"They shouldn't," replied Vanover. "No food for them this deep. But old Clarence, he's never been your average hunk of seafood. I'm going to set us down on the bottom. Play dead. See if he'll leave us alone."

He worked the joystick, and the submersible banked away from Clarence's next assault. As the ballast tanks expelled air, the vehicle fell abruptly, stabilized, and dropped again, catching the edge of the shelf a few hundred yards past the shipwreck. It bounced once and then plowed to a lurching halt in the wet mud and sand.

Inside the cabin, the shaken crew of five waited breathlessly. What would Clarence do now?

The big shark circled them at a distance, its streamlined eighteen-foot body blinking in and out of the reach of *Deep Scout's* floodlights.

Go away, thought Kaz, trying to will his message through the pressurized bubble. *Once was a fluke, but now you're stalking me!*

The speaker crackled to life, and they all jumped. "*Scout*, this is topside. Braden, I'm reading you at a dead stop at seven-oh-three. Just checking to make sure that's where you want to be."

Clarence was closer now, still orbiting them, crescent tail sculling lazily. "It's a long story, topside," the captain replied. "But we're okay here. Out."

"Are we okay?" Dante asked nervously.

The shark approached from the left, sizing up the submersible with glassy, dispassionate eyes. The mouth was slightly open now, and they could see past the ranks of razor-sharp knives clear into the beast's gullet. And then, without warning, the great predator turned on a dime and disappeared into the blackness.

No one spoke. No one dared. It was almost as if saying the words aloud — *he's gone* — might bring the monster back upon them. For several minutes, there was no sound but the hiss of oxygen, punctuated by the pinging of *Deep Scout*'s beacon.

Vanover picked himself up off the deck. "Now, let's see if we can snag ourselves a piece of treasure."

"Yeah!" cheered Dante. "We're still right on schedule! Come on, baby, give us some *gold*."

THE DEEP

The others ignored him. They had noticed what Dante had not — that while the captain vigorously worked the controls, nothing was happening.

Vanover continued to fill the ballast tanks with air, but the submersible did not lift off the ledge. "Uh-oh."

"Uh-oh?" echoed Adriana. "What do you mean, uh-oh?"

The captain spoke into the microphone. "Topside, this is *Scout*. I've got two full ballast tanks, but she won't budge off the bottom. Can you see any problems from your end?"

The small speaker crackled with the reply. "Negative, Braden. All your readings are normal. Are your thrusters functioning?"

"That's a yes, topside. Request permission to abort mission and drop weights for a quick ascent."

"Abort the mission?" repeated Dante. "But we need a piece of the treasure to take to court!"

"Forget the treasure," Kaz said sharply. "It won't do us much good if we're stuck under seven hundred feet of ocean."

The submersible shuddered as the heavy lead weights dropped to the mud of the shelf. The interns held their breath. *Deep Scout* didn't budge.

It was the first moment that Star felt real fear.

The incident with Clarence had been unnerving, but she had known all along that no shark, not even an eighteen-footer, could penetrate the submersible's husk. But to be trapped on the seafloor in a titanium coffin — that was far more terrifying. Oh, sure, a heavy salvage ship could reach them with a crane eventually. But such vessels were slow and ungainly. It would take hours, even days, to get one in place above them.

She posed the question, although she dreaded the answer almost as much as the awful fate it would surely foretell. "Captain, how much air do we have left?"

"Just under eleven hours," he replied. "That's if you believe the instruments. And according to them, we should be on the surface by now."

"You mean we're *stuck* here?" cried Adriana. "For how long?"

"Anything more than eleven hours may as well be forever," Star pointed out.

"What about these?" asked Dante, indicating a rack of six miniature compressed-air tanks. "We're not stuck. We can swim out!"

Star shook her head. "Not from seven hundred feet. The pressure's more than twenty atmospheres at this depth. Popping that hatch would be suicide. The water would come in hard enough to crush us."

"So there's nothing we can do?" Adriana couldn't believe it. "We just wait around to *suffocate*?"

"Nobody's suffocating," said Vanover through clenched teeth. He fired the rear thrusters, struggling to point the vehicle's snub nose upward. There was a loud grinding sound; the sub shuddered. And then *Deep Scout* lurched clumsily off the muddy shelf, beginning a slow, angled climb.

The cheering in the tiny cabin was deafening.

"Quiet!" barked the captain. Into the microphone, he said, "Topside, this is *Scout*. We're going to need divers in the water. Repeat: divers — as many as you can spare. This is not a drill."

"What's wrong, Captain?" asked Star. "You fixed the problem. We're on our way up."

Vanover pointed to the temperature gauge on the data screen. It read 44.7 degrees Fahrenheit. "The temp should be going up as we climb into warmer water."

Adriana regarded the readout. "It's not changing."

"The probe is in the belly of the sub, behind two fiberglass plates," the captain explained. "I think those plates separated, and we scooped up a load of mud when we landed on the shelf. That's why the temp is staying low — it's packed in cold mud."

"The shark!" Kaz exclaimed suddenly. "Clarence must have separated those plates when he rammed the hull!"

"However it happened," Vanover went on, "it wouldn't take more than half a ton of muck to throw off our whole ballasting system. *Deep Scout's* a simple boat. She sinks when she's heavy; she rises when she's light. The thrusters are just for maneuvering." He took a deep breath. "We're not going to make it all the way to the surface on thruster power alone."

CHAPTER SEVENTEEN

Star stared at the captain in alarm. "There must be *something* we can do!"

"Everybody strap on an air tank," Vanover ordered. "I'm going to bring her as high as she'll go. When the thrusters start to fail, I'll blow the hatch, and we'll swim for the surface." He turned to the microphone. "Topside, did you catch any of that?"

"Affirmative, Braden," crackled the speaker. "My divers are dressing out right now."

Star showed the others how to strap the small wing tanks to their arms. *It's unreal,* she thought to herself. *I'm so scared I want to throw up.* And yet, outwardly, she seemed totally unruffled, dispensing calm, efficient advice to her companions. "When we're about to crack the hatch, pinch your nose and blow, like you're clearing your ears on a dive. Otherwise, the pressure jump will bust your eardrums." She affixed the last cylinder to the captain's burly arm.

Kaz, Adriana, and Dante nodded, mute with shock and dread.

The steady hiss of air suddenly jumped to a roar.

DIVE

"I'm bleeding as much gas as I can into the cabin," Vanover explained, "building up our pressure so the water doesn't crush us."

Star kept one eye on the Fathometer readout. They were passing through four hundred feet.

Still too deep. To stand a fighting chance, they'd need to reach two hundred.

One-fifty would be better.

The sub was vibrating dangerously as the captain fought to pull the vehicle out of the ocean's abyss. *He's right,* she realized. The weak thrusters weren't designed to bring *Deep Scout* back to the surface — and certainly not when the submersible was weighted down with a half ton of mud.

The question is: How high can we get?

Three hundred feet. "Come on, girl," grunted Vanover, bathed in sweat. "Don't quit on me now."

As they passed through 250 feet, the black of the ocean subtly morphed into an ultraviolet indigo. Proof that the sun was up there somewhere, far above them.

"Divers in the water," came the report through the tinny speaker.

"Pray we'll have work for them," Vanover said grimly.

Two hundred and twenty feet. The first thruster

failed and *Deep Scout* began to veer left, unable to maintain a steady course.

"Everybody flat on the deck!" the captain ordered. "When the sea comes in, it'll bounce us around like Ping-Pong balls!"

As the interns struggled to arrange themselves on the tiny available floor space, the submersible went into a spin, crushing them together.

Vanover clung to the joystick like it was the saddle horn of a bucking bronco. "Ready to blow the hatch!"

Star risked one last look at the Fathometer: 206 feet. Were they high enough?

She never saw the hatch actually open. It was just gone, and Niagara Falls was roaring into *Deep Scout*. She pinched her nostrils and blew hard, but her ears still exploded with pain as nearly seven atmospheres of pressure brought the ocean down upon them. The impact was crushing, a full body blow that plastered her against the deck. The captain was swept out of his chair and flung into the heavy acrylic of the sphere.

Then, all at once, the tempest was over. *Deep Scout's* cabin was filled with icy water — at two hundred feet, even a tropical sea was cold. Shivering, Star bit down on her regulator and began pushing the others through the open hatch. The nitrogen narcosis hit her almost immediately —

an instant, pleasant wooziness that eased the chill and the salt sting in her unprotected eyes. *It makes sense,* she reasoned. *I'm breathing compressed air at incredible depth.*

Kaz was fouled in some wires that had become exposed when the onslaught of the sea had wrenched the data screen free of the control console. Star got him untangled and barked, "Go!" into her regulator, following his clumsy progress out of the vehicle. She hoped the others could figure out that they had to find the surface now. Surely they were just as narced as she was.

Star watched as Dante, Adriana, and finally Kaz began to kick upward. Exhaling a bubbly sigh of relief, Star followed. Yet through her nitrogen haze, she couldn't escape the feeling that she'd forgotten something important, left a key task undone.

As she rose, a shape drifted out of *Deep Scout* twenty feet below her. Arms outstretched, it began to sink slowly.

The realization burned through the fog like brilliant sun: *The captain!*

She did a U-turn in the water, diving against her body's natural buoyancy. With no weight belt, descent was difficult. She kicked hard against the sea's resistance, her compact form tight and vector straight. Fighting the rules of physics, she closed the gap between herself and Vanover. Fifteen feet . . . ten . . . five . . . almost there . . .

That was when she realized that no bubbles were coming from his nose or mouth. The captain was dead.

His eyes were closed. He must have been knocked unconscious when the surging water slammed him against the sphere. His tank was gone too, probably ripped away by the same irresistible force. The laws of science and pressure — harmless and boring on a piece of paper in diving class. But here in real life — brutal, overpowering, deadly.

She grabbed his arm. It was lifeless, a piece of floating debris. There was one more chance. She pulled out her regulator and forced it between his gray lips.

Nothing. The man was gone.

She screamed with grief and sorrow, and didn't stop until her own choking extinguished her voice.

Convulsed with coughs, she didn't notice the explosion of bubbles soaring upward from her regulator.

Oh, no! The demand valve!

By the time she bit down on the mouthpiece, she knew that most of the air supply had already escaped. Only deep, wheezing pulls would draw anything from the cylinder. Below two hundred feet, gas went fast, compressed by the depth.

I've got to get out of here!

She shot for the surface, careful not to ascend faster than her slowest bubbles. She got two more gulps of air before the tank went empty, and she swallowed hard to force back her thirst for more.

Don't hold your breath, she reminded herself. That was a good way to rupture a lung. All gasses expand on the way up, including the ones already in your pulmonary system.

One hundred and fifty feet. *Hang in there!* She knew she might get another inhalation if she could make it to one hundred — the traces of air in the tank would expand to provide one more suck. She checked her watch — 120 feet — and —

Right there, rising out of the bowels of the ocean, her heart stopped. Beside the Fathometer reading, a single word flashed on and off, accompanied by a high-pitched beeping.

DECOMP.

Decompression. She had spent too much time at depth. It was no longer safe for her to return to the surface without stopping to give her body a chance to expel nitrogen.

But I can't stop! I'm out of air!

THE DEEP

CHAPTER EIGHTEEN

It was every diver's worst nightmare. The choice that was really no choice at all. Ascend to the surface and risk the harmful, even deadly effects of the bends.

Or drown.

Star made the decision in a split second. It was no contest. Drowning was a sure thing. *I'll take my chances with the bends!*

Upward she soared, her feet kicking like pistons. As she passed through eighty feet, she managed to squeeze another fraction of a breath out of her empty tank. Then she swallowed again, fighting back the craving of her lungs. It was illogical, but she could almost feel the nitrogen bubbles frothing her blood into a milk shake as she rose to warmth and light.

No thinking, she exhorted herself. *Swim!*

Star broke through the waves to a world she'd thought she might never see again. Two huge gulps of air — pure heaven — and then the important business of yelling for help. "Hey! Hey!!"

Gasping, she tried to orient herself. The steely

bulk of *Scoutmaster's* stern loomed about fifty yards away.

Strong hands grasped her from behind, and she cried out in shock.

"It's okay!" the rescue diver soothed her. "I'm here to help. Don't worry — it's over."

"It's not over!" she shrieked. "I'm bent!"

"You weren't down long enough," he assured her. "You came straight up."

"I *didn't!*" she insisted. "I tried to save the captain! He didn't make it! Look!" She held her watch under his nose.

The man took one look at the flashing DECOMP signal and spoke into the transmitter in his hood. "Topside, this is Diver Two. I need a chopper evac to decompression — now!" He regarded Star intently. "The captain — where did you see him and how long ago?"

"He was sinking from two hundred," she gasped, fighting hysteria. Sharp pains stung her hips and knees. Nitrogen bubbles, collecting in her joints — classic symptoms of the bends. "He wasn't moving, wasn't breathing. I tried to give him my air —" She began to shiver with cold, the onset of shock. *Hold it together. . . .*

The diver grabbed her gently but firmly and began to kick for *Scoutmaster.*

Staring straight up into the blinding sun, Star wept bitter tears. She couldn't tell if she was crying for the captain or for herself. It was all the same tragedy. A good man was gone forever, and she was face-to-face with the possibility that this accident was going to end her life, right here, today.

And then she was being hauled aboard, first to a dive platform, and then onto *Scoutmaster's* deck.

She looked up, her vision blurred, and saw Kaz — two of him, actually.

"I'm sorry!" she sobbed.

"For what?" he asked. "Are you okay? Where's the captain?"

"Dead!"

"That's not funny, Star!" It was Dante, with Adriana at his side. "Hey, you don't look so hot — "

"I tried to help him. I stayed too long. I'm *bent!*"

She was having trouble breathing now, struggling under what felt like a boulder on her chest.

She was aware of a lot of frantic activity before someone slipped an oxygen mask over her nose and mouth. Faces flashed through her pain, those of her three companions and others too. The last thing she heard before slipping into unconsciousness was the distant rhythm of an approaching helicopter.

For Kaz, the nightmare was happening again. He stood on deck in his dripping shorts and T-shirt, watching the crew preparing Star's inert body for airlift. It brought him back to a hockey rink, not so many months ago. Drew Christiansen on a stretcher. The ambulance, backing in the Zamboni entrance. And the siren.

Today, that mournful wail was replaced by the thunder of the chopper as it hovered over them, lowering its wire-mesh recovery cage for Star.

Star. How can this be happening to her? She's the best of all of us!

He choked back tears as he watched the crew lay her down on the padded bottom of the basket. She had saved his life that day. He would not have made it out of *Deep Scout* without her help untangling the wires that had trapped him.

He was here; he was fine. And she —

The crew backed away, and the cage lifted off. Kaz was suddenly overwhelmed by the sheer loneliness of Star's journey — one from which she might never return. Almost before he knew what he was doing, he was running forward. He put both hands on the rim of the basket and vaulted over the side, landing neatly next to her.

Everyone aboard *Scoutmaster* — the interns and crew alike — was shouting at him. But the roar of the chopper drowned them out. The basket was winched up through the windstorm of the rotor blades and hauled into the cabin.

No time was wasted. The helicopter was racing to its destination even before the hatch was closed.

The paramedic glared at Kaz. "Not smart, kid. You think this is a game?"

"I couldn't let her go alone," mumbled Kaz, holding on to Star's limp hand.

The craft was only in the air eleven minutes. Kaz watched in awe as they closed in on an enormous oil-drilling platform off the west coast of Saint-Luc. When they descended toward the helipad, he got a sense of the vast size of the structure. It was like an entire city, propped up on titanic stilts, hundreds of feet above the Caribbean.

A medical team was waiting for them at touchdown. Kaz joined the stampede with the stretcher. An elevator took them into the guts of the platform, where the infirmary was located.

The double doors were marked RECOMPRESSION THERAPY. A dour-faced, lab-coated technician barred their way.

"She can't come in here. I've got hard-hat

divers in the water. What if one of them needs — "

Before the man could finish, Bobby Kaczinski, the most promising young defenseman in the Ontario Minor Hockey Association, did what he had been trained to do his entire life. Without slowing his pace, he lowered his shoulder and delivered a crunching body check that put the technician flat on his back.

The decompression chamber looked like a huge high-tech steel pipe about the size of a Dumpster.

Kaz got out of the way as the medical team worked on Star. She was hooked up to various monitors, and an IV drip was started. The oxygen was discontinued, and adrenaline administered.

This isn't happening . . . this isn't Star . . . this isn't our summer. . . .

The heavy door swung shut, rubber gaskets muffling the clang of metal on metal. The hyperbaric chamber pressed Star and a nurse down to seven atmospheres — the same pressure as 228 feet. According to the dive computer in Star's watch, that was the maximum depth of her unplanned adventure. Over the next several hours, that pressure would be slowly reduced, giving her system a chance to expel the nitrogen that was overwhelming her body.

But was the damage already done? It had

THE DEEP

taken half an hour to get her into the chamber. Thirty minutes of deadly bubbles foaming her blood.

He looked to the chief doctor, but the man's face revealed no clue as to how the treatment was proceeding.

This is what we get for trespassing on the graves of sailors who've been dead for three hundred years.

First the captain, and now Star. It was too much to bear.

Two hours later, when Adriana and Dante rushed into the infirmary, the doctor's expression had not changed.

"She's okay, right?" Dante asked eagerly. "Is she okay?"

Kaz just shook his head and directed their attention to the chamber's window. There lay their friend, her face chalk-white, still unconscious.

The double doors swung wide to reveal Menasce Gérard, terrible in his anger and grief.

"This is true, this thing I hear?" he demanded, voice booming. "The captain?"

"He's dead," Adriana confirmed in a husky whisper. "Star tried to save him and she — "

The big dive guide strode to the window in the chamber. His fury softened at the sight of Star, and he placed a hand against the glass, as if trying to project his strength across the space between them. Then he wheeled and faced down the other three.

"*Alors* — here is your treasure! Are you happy now? Do you feel rich?"

They could not argue, nor defend themselves. They could only wait.

THE DEEP

02 September 1665

The Griffin *under full sail was a majestic sight. She was a barque, three-masted, carrying twenty-four guns, and built low to the water, much different from the workhorses of the Spanish treasure fleet. The galleons were massive, with towering decks. Loaded down with their precious cargoes, they wallowed in the sea, sitting ducks for the faster, more maneuverable ships of the great naval powers — England, France, Holland. And, of course, the pirates and corsairs.*

That was why Captain Blade was not overly concerned about the four-day head start the Spaniards had on the privateer fleet.

"We'll overtake them, we will!" Samuel heard him boast to his officers. Under torture, the mayor of Portobelo had revealed the route the fleet would be following back to Spain. There would be no usual stop in Havana. Instead, the galleons would veer to the south, picking their way through the notorious Hidden Shoals.

DIVE

As the privateer fleet navigated this course, Captain Blade ringed his vessel with lookouts and placed dozens of men in the highest rigging to scan the horizon for sails. Even when the skies darkened four days later and the rains came, he would not allow them to abandon their posts.

The next morning, with eighteen-foot waves crashing over the bowsprit, gunner's mate Blankenship was hurled from the mizzenmast as the barque heeled in the violent seas.

Even York felt the need to plead with the captain for the safety of the crew. "Sir, the ratlines are not fit for man nor beast with the sea in this condition! We've lost one already!"

"And we'll lose many more," Blade predicted. "That's what the scum are for. Better to lose a few hands than the Spanish fleet!"

Samuel, who was cleaning up the captain's breakfast dishes and stumbling on the unsteady deck, exclaimed, "But sir — "

York silenced him with a sharp slap across the mouth.

It stung, but Samuel realized the barber had just done him a favor. For if the man had given Blade a chance to deliver the blow himself, it surely would have come from the bone-handled snake whip.

"Captain," York persisted, "what might a lookout

THE DEEP

spy in such weather? Do you not know the size and nature of this storm?"

"That I do," agreed Blade. "'Tis a monster gale stretching a hundred miles in all directions around a pinhole of clear blue sky. Aye, that's the beauty part."

Samuel could not contain himself. "Beauty? Such storms destroy ships, with all hands lost!"

"Perchance they do," Blade acknowledged. "But if we're in it, so are the Spaniards." He emitted a diabolical cackle. "Die we might, boy. But if we live, by God, we'll all be filthy rich!"

ABOUT THE AUTHOR

GORDON KORMAN is the author of more than forty books for children and young adults, including the Island series and the Everest series, as well as *The Chicken Doesn't Skate*, the Slapshots series, and *Liar, Liar, Pants on Fire*. He lives on Long Island with his wife and children.

Deep, deep danger!

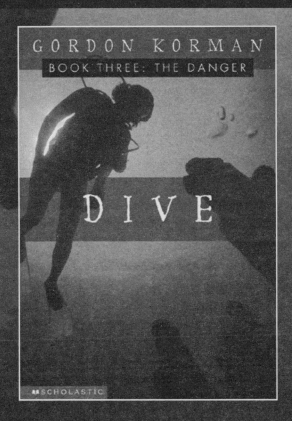

GORDON KORMAN

BOOK THREE: THE DANGER

DIVE

■SCHOLASTIC

If someone has to get the treasure, who will it be—Kaz, Star, Adriana, Dante, or the adults who think they'll steal it for themselves? Can friendships survive the pressure when the stakes are higher than ever?

All the questions are answered in this stunning finale.

■SCHOLASTIC

Adventure X 3!

From best-selling author **Gordon Korman**

The rules have just
been swept away…

Four friends. One mountain.
Only one can be first.